THE LADY . . . OR THE TIGER?

When he turned and looked at her, he saw that she knew behind which door crouched the tiger, and behind which stood the lady. The only hope for the youth was based upon the success of the princess in discovering the mystery.

Then it was that his quick and anxious glance asked the question, "Which?"

She raised her hand, and made a slight, quick movement to the right. No one saw her. Every eye was fixed on the man in the arena.

He turned, and with a firm and rapid step he walked across the empty space. Every heart stopped beating, every breath was held . . .

He went to the door on the right, and opened it . . .

THE LADY OR THE TIGER

AND OTHER STORIES

Frank Stockton

TOR®

A TOM DOHERTY ASSOCIATES BOOK
NEW YORK

This is a work of fiction. All the characters and events portrayed in this book are fictitious, and any resemblance to real people or events is purely coincidental.

THE LADY OR THE TIGER AND OTHER STORIES BY FRANK STOCKTON

Cover art by David Heffernan

A Tor Book
Published by Tom Doherty Associates, LLC
175 Fifth Avenue
New York, NY 10010

www.tor.com

Tor® is a registered trademark of Tom Doherty Associates, LLC.

ISBN: 0-812-51956-6

First Tor edition: April 1992

Printed in the United States of America

0 9 8 7 6 5 4 3

Table of Contents

Contents

The Life of Frank Stockton

Frances Richard Stockton was born a lame and delicate child on April 5, 1834. As a youngster, Frank entertained his numerous brothers and sisters with stories as soon as he could talk. In fact, while walking to school he would "take up the thread of a story and carry it on from day to day until the thing became a serial."

Trained as an engraver, he started a shop with his brother John in the early 1850s after graduation from high school. The two of them were able to support themselves from the beginning with commissions from magazines and newspapers. While Frank was not a great artist, he was good enough to make a living at it, and interested enough in the field to invent and patent an engraving tool that cut parallel lines at the same time. With this tool he illustrated a book, *Poems*, written by John.

But although wood engraving was what he knew best, storytelling was his first love. Since his early days of frail health he had written stories and fairy tales for himself. He had even won some prizes at school for his literary efforts. So right after graduation, he began submitting his stories to newspapers and magazines, collecting scores of rejection letters along the way. But he was persistent and, when he was scarcely twenty, his first story finally appeared in the *Philadelphia Courier* newspaper. "The Slight

Mistake," as it was called was, according to Stockton himself, "an imitation of Dumas and other favorite French authors."

By the time Frank Stockton had reached his mid-thirties, he was successful enough to give up the wood engraving business and concentrate on his literary efforts. However, he was cautious enough not to try and make his living entirely from writing, joining the staff of the magazine *Hearth and Home* under the editorship of the amazing Mary Mapes Dodge. Later when Mrs. Dodge began the children's magazine *St. Nicholas*—the most important magazine ever published for young readers—Stockton went along to serve as her assistant.

Stockton met his wife, Mary Ann Edwards Tuttle, at the West Philadelphia School for Young Ladies where she was teaching English. The head of the school was Stockton's mother, and he was a frequent visitor there.

Mary Ann was a Southerner from South Carolina, so during the Civil War years she and Stockton moved to New Jersey, as far away as they could from war activities. They engaged in almost no political activities, though Stockton did write and have privately published "A Northern Voice for the Dissolution of the Union" which he quickly withdrew when Fort Sumter was fired upon. But New Jersey during the war years was not a fertile place for Stockton and he wrote no fiction the entire time he was there.

In 1868, having moved back to Philadelphia with Mary Ann, Stockton became a regular contributor to a variety of magazines, including the *Riverside Magazine*, one of the most important of the time. And when Mary Mapes Dodge began *Hearth and*

Home in that same year, it was as if Frank Stockton had truly discovered his calling. From then on his writing appeared regularly, both stories and articles. He wrote so much, in fact, that he often wrote pieces under pen names—Paul Fort and John Lewees were two of them—when the magazines needed padding out.

His first book for children was a collection of tales about a tiny fairy named Ting-a-ling. Initially published as individual stories in *Riverside Magazine*, the book came out in 1870. It was then Stockton gave up the engraving business for good. About *Ting-a-ling*, he wrote: "I was determined to write fairy tales because my mind was full of them."

A very prolific writer, Stockton overworked himself back into ill health. This time his eyes began to fail. Several vacations helped for a bit, but when he returned to work, his eyes were as bad as before. In 1876 he was forced to resign from *St. Nicholas* and concentrate only on his writing.

By this time he and his wife were once again living in New Jersey, on a comfortable farm, and Stockton adopted a new method of working that seemed more idyll than occupation. In the summers he would lie in a hammock under the trees with a stenographer (often Mary Ann) sitting nearby. She would also have a book with her to keep her occupied while the author was thinking. Once he had the story thoroughly worked out, he would call her over and tell it rapidly. (In the winter they moved the whole writing process indoors by the hearthfire.) This prone method of writing was dictated by Stockton's ill health, but while he had been forced to give up his work on the magazines, he had not forsaken his love for the stimulating intellectual conversations he had found while working there. So he spent a part of each winter in New York City, visiting the various clubs to which he belonged. Many of the adult stories he wrote dealt with genteel and sophisticated New Yorkers, and with his engaging and cosmopolitan wit Stockton was a popular man.

In 1882 he wrote his most famous story, "The Lady and the Tiger." His life was changed from the moment of its publication. With its surprise ending, the story was a hit from the first. It had been written for a reading at a literary society and when they heard it, the club members spent so much time discussing it that Stockton was determined to get it published. It came out in the November 1882 edition of *The Century Magazine*. Within months, it was known worldwide, being argued in debating societies and lectured on from pulpits. Stockton had rewritten the ending five different times and got so tired of answering the question of which was behind the door, he took to answering: "If you decide which it was—the lady or the tiger—you find out what kind of person you are yourself."

He died on April 20, 1902, at age sixty-nine, in Washington, D.C. where he had gone to attend a dinner of the National Academy of Sciences. He became ill at the dinner and had to be carried back to his hotel where he died four days later of a cerebral hemorrhage.

—Jane Yolen

Foreword

For seventy years, between November 1873 and June 1943, the world's finest magazine for children was published: *St. Nicholas, A Monthly Magazine for Boys and Girls.* For the first thirty-two of those years the magazine's editor was Mary Mapes Dodge, a creative and strong-minded woman who was the author of the childhood classic *Hans Brinker: or the Silver Skates.*

A young widow with two sons, Mary Mapes Dodge had been the editor of *Hearth and Home* for five years when the directors of Scribner's & Sons asked her to start a children's magazine. She was delighted to do so as long as she could make it, in her words, a child's "pleasure-ground."

She chose Frank Stockton as her assistant. Already known to her from his work on the staff of *Hearth and Home* as well as for his wonderful children's stories, Stockton was the perfect choice. When his health gave way three years later, she was devastated, but they remained friends until his death in 1902.

The magazine began with forty-eight pages, but quickly grew to double that size. At year's end, the twelve issues were often bound up in two leather or buckram volumes by libraries or collectors.

From the beginning the magazine managed to attract the best of the children's book authors and illustrators. Rudyard Kipling's *Just So* and *Jungle Books* stories appeared in *St. Nicholas*, as did Howard Pyle's fairy tales, Laura E. Richard's poetry, and serialized novels like Louisa May Alcott's *Jo's Boys*, Lucretia Hale's *The Peterkin Papers*, and Howard Pyle's *The Story of King Arthur*. Authors of adult books, like Mark Twain, and poets Longfellow and William Cullen Bryant also sent work. In fact, the table of contents read like a who's who of literature at the time.

Mary Mapes Dodge proclaimed her editorial policy in ringing tones:

To give clean, genuine fun to children of all ages.

To give them examples of the finest types of boyhood and girlhood.

To inspire them with a fine appreciation of pictorial art.

To cultivate the imagination in profitable directions.

To foster a love of country, home, nature, truth, beauty, sincerity.

To prepare boys and girls for life as it is.

To stimulate their ambitions—but along normally progressive lines.

To keep pace with a fast-moving world in all its activities.

To give reading matter which every parent may pass to his children unhesitatingly.

It was a policy—and a promise—the magazine was to keep for seventy years.

Foreword

Another of the original and interesting aspects of the magazine was the St. Nicholas League, begun in 1898, which offered gold and silver badges for children who sent in excellent pieces of writing that were picked for publication.

Among the well-known writers whose very first works were published when they were children in the League were Ring Lardner, Edna St. Vincent Millay, Cornelia Otis Skinner, Stephen Vincent Benet, Bennet Cerf, and Edmund Wilson, among others. *St. Nicholas* was an actual training ground for several generations of important American writers.

Although *St. Nicholas* died in 1939, and was fitfully revived until its final issue in 1943, it is still the standard for all children's magazines. It was the one place where, a critic said, "majors wrote for minors."

—Jane Yolen

The Lady,
or the Tiger?

IN THE very olden time there lived a semibarbaric
king, whose ideas, though somewhat polished
and sharpened by the progressiveness of distant
Latin neighbors, were still large, florid, and untram-
melled, as became the half of him which was barbaric. He was a man of exuberant fancy, and, withal,
of an authority so irresistible that, at his will, he
turned his varied fancies into facts. He was greatly
given to self-communing; and when he and himself
agreed upon anything, the thing was done. When
every member of his domestic and political systems
moved smoothly in its appointed course, his nature
was bland and genial; but whenever there was a little hitch, and some of his orbs got out of their or-
bits, he was blander and more genial still, for
nothing pleased him so much as to make the
crooked straight, and crush down uneven places.

Among the borrowed notions by which his barbarism had become semified was that of the public arena, in which, by exhibitions of manly and beastly valor, the minds of his subjects were refined and cultured.

But even here the exuberant and barbaric fancy asserted itself. The arena of the king was built not to give the people an opportunity of hearing the rhapsodies of dying gladiators, nor to enable them to view the inevitable conclusion of a conflict between religious opinions and hungry jaws, but for purposes far better adapted to widen and develop the mental energies of the people. This vast amphitheatre, with its encircling galleries, its mysterious vaults, and its unseen passages, was an agent of poetic justice, in which crime was punished, or virtue rewarded, by the decrees of an impartial and incorruptible chance.

When a subject was accused of a crime of sufficient importance to interest the king, public notice was given that on an appointed day the fate of the accused person would be decided in the king's arena—a structure which well deserved its name; for, although its form and plan were borrowed from afar, its purpose emanated solely from the brain of this man, who, every barleycorn a king, knew no tradition to which he owed more allegiance than pleased his fancy, and who ingrafted on every adopted form of human thought and action the rich growth of his barbaric idealism.

When all the people had assembled in the galleries, and the king, surrounded by his court, sat high up on his throne of royal state on one side of the arena, he gave a signal, a door beneath him opened, and the accused subject stepped out into the amphitheatre. Directly opposite him, on the other side of the enclosed space, were two doors, exactly alike and side by side. It was the duty and the privilege of the person on trial to walk directly to these doors and open one of them. He could open either door he pleased: he was subject to no guidance or influence but that of the afore-mentioned impartial and incorruptible chance. If he opened the one, there came out of it a hungry tiger, the fiercest and most cruel that could be procured, which immediately sprang upon him and tore him to pieces, as a punishment for his guilt. The moment that the case of the criminal was thus decided, doleful iron bells were clanged, great wails went up from the hired mourners posted on the outer rim of the arena, and the vast audience, with bowed heads and downcast hearts, wended slowly their homeward way, mourning greatly that one so young and fair, or so old and respected, should have merited so dire a fate.

But if the accused person opened the other door, there came forth from it a lady, the most suitable to his years and station that his Majesty could select among his fair subjects; and to this lady he was immediately married, as a reward of his innocence. It mattered not that he might already possess a wife and family, or that his affections might be engaged upon an object of his own selection: the king allowed no such subordinate arrangements to interfere with his great scheme of retribution and reward. The exercises, as in the other instance, took place immediately, and in the arena. Another door opened beneath the king, and a priest, followed by a band of choristers, and dancing maidens blowing joyous airs on golden horns and treading an epithalamic measure, advanced to where the pair stood side by side; and the wedding was promptly and cheerily solemnized. Then the gay brass bells rang forth their merry peals, the people shouted glad hurrahs, and the innocent man, preceded by children strewing flowers on his path, led his bride to his home.

This was the king's semibarbaric method of administering justice. Its perfect fairness is obvious. The criminal could not know out of which door would come the lady: he opened either he pleased, without having the slightest idea whether, in the next instant, he was to be devoured or married. On some occasions the tiger came out of one door, and on some out of the other. The decisions of this tribunal were not only fair, they were positively determinate: the accused person was instantly punished if he found himself guilty; and if innocent, he was rewarded on the spot, whether he liked it or not. There was no escape from the judgments of the king's arena.

The institution was a very popular one. When the people gathered together on one of the great trial-days, they never knew whether they were to witness a bloody slaughter or a hilarious wedding. This element of uncertainty lent an interest to the occasion which it could not otherwise have attained. Thus the masses were entertained and pleased, and the thinking part of the community could bring no charge of unfairness against this plan; for did not the accused person have the whole matter in his own hands?

This semibarbaric king had a daughter as blooming as his most florid fancies, and with a soul as fervent and imperious as his own. As is usual in such cases, she was the apple of his eye, and was loved by him above all humanity. Among his courtiers was a young man of that fineness of blood and lowness of station common to the conventional heroes of romance who love royal maidens. This royal maiden was well satisfied with her lover, for he was handsome and brave to a degree unsurpassed in all this kingdom; and she loved him with an ardor that had enough of barbarism in it to make it exceedingly warm and strong. This love-affair moved on happily for many months, until one day the king happened to discover its existence. He did not hesitate nor waver in regard to his duty in the premises. The youth was immediately cast into prison, and a day was appointed for his trial in the king's arena. This, of course, was an especially important occasion; and his Majesty, as well as all the people, were greatly interested in the workings and development of this trial. Never before had such a case occurred; never before had a subject dared to love the daughter of a king. In afteryears such things became commonplace enough; but then they were, in no slight degree, novel and startling.

The tiger-cages of the kingdom were searched for the most savage and relentless beasts, from which the fiercest monster might be selected for the arena; and the ranks of maiden youth and beauty throughout the land were carefully surveyed by competent judges, in order that the young man might have a fitting bride in case fate did not determine for him a different destiny. Of course everybody knew that the deed with which the accused was charged had been done. He had loved the princess, and neither he, she, nor any one else thought of denying the fact; but the king would not think of allowing any fact of this kind to interfere with the workings of the tribunal, in which he took such great delight and satisfaction. No matter how the affair turned out, the youth would be disposed of; and the king would take an æsthetic pleasure in watching the course of events, which would determine whether or not the young man had done wrong in allowing himself to love the princess.

The appointed day arrived. From far and near the

people gathered, and thronged the great galleries of the arena; and crowds, unable to gain admittance, massed themselves against its outside walls. The king and his court were in their places, opposite the twin doors—those fateful portals, so terrible in their similarity.

All was ready. The signal was given. A door beneath the royal party opened, and the lover of the princess walked into the arena. Tall, beautiful, fair, his appearance was greeted with a low hum of admiration and anxiety. Half the audience had not known so grand a youth had lived among them. No wonder the princess loved him! What a terrible thing for him to be there!

As the youth advanced into the arena, he turned, as the custom was, to bow to the king: but he did not think at all of that royal personage; his eyes were fixed upon the princess, who sat to the right of her father. Had it not been for the moiety of barbarism in her nature it is probable that lady would not have been there; but her intense and fervid soul would not allow her to be absent on an occasion in which she was so terribly interested. From the moment that the decree had gone forth that her lover should decide his fate in the king's arena, she had thought of nothing, night or day, but this great event and the various subjects connected with it. Possessed of more power, influence, and force of character than any one who had ever before been interested in such a case, she had done what no other person had done—she had possessed herself of the secret of the doors. She knew in which of the two rooms that lay behind those doors stood the cage of the tiger, with its open front, and in which waited the lady. Through these thick doors, heavily curtained with skins on the inside, it was impossible that any noise or suggestion should come from within to the person who should approach to raise the latch of one of them; but gold, and the power of a woman's will, had brought the secret to the princess.

And not only did she know in which room stood the lady ready to emerge, all blushing and radiant, should her door be opened, but she knew who the lady was. It was one of the fairest and loveliest of the damsels of the court who had been selected as the reward of the accused youth, should he be proved innocent of the crime of aspiring to one so far above him; and the princess hated her. Often had she seen, or imagined that she had seen, this fair creature throwing glances of admiration upon the person of her lover, and sometimes she thought these glances were perceived and even returned. Now and then she had seen them talking together; it was but for a moment or two, but much can be said in a brief space; it may have been on most unimportant topics, but how could she know that? The girl was lovely, but she had dared to raise her eyes to the loved one of the princess; and, with all the intensity of the savage blood transmitted to her through long lines of wholly barbaric ancestors, she hated the woman who blushed and trembled behind that silent door.

When her lover turned and looked at her, and his eye met hers as she sat there paler and whiter than any one in the vast ocean of anxious faces about her, he saw, by that power of quick perception which is given to those whose souls are one, that she knew behind which door crouched the tiger, and behind which stood the lady. He had expected her to know it. He understood her nature, and his soul was assured that she would never rest until she had made plain to herself this thing, hidden to all other lookers-on, even to the king. The only hope for the youth in which there was any element of certainty was based upon the success of the princess in discovering this mystery; and the moment he looked upon her, he saw she had succeeded, as in his soul he knew she would succeed.

Then it was that his quick and anxious glance asked the question, "Which?" It was as plain to her as if he shouted it from where he stood. There was not an instant to be lost. The question was asked in a flash; it must be answered in another.

Her right arm lay on the cushioned parapet before her. She raised her hand, and made a slight, quick movement toward the right. No one but her lover saw her. Every eye but his was fixed on the man in the arena.

He turned, and with a firm and rapid step he walked across the empty space. Every heart stopped beating, every breath was held, every eye was fixed immovably upon that man. Without the slightest hesitation, he went to the door on the right, and opened it.

Now, the point of the story is this: Did the tiger come out of that door, or did the lady?

The more we reflect upon this question the harder it is to answer. It involves a study of the human heart which leads us through devious mazes of passion, out of which it is difficult to find our way. Think of it, fair reader, not as if the decision of the question depended upon yourself, but upon that hot-blooded, semibarbaric princess, her soul at a white heat beneath the combined fires of despair and jealousy. She had lost him, but who should have him?

How often, in her waking hours and in her dreams, had she started in wild horror and covered her face with her hands as she thought of her lover opening the door on the other side of which waited the cruel fangs of the tiger!

But how much oftener had she seen him at the other door! How in her grievous reveries had she gnashed her teeth and torn her hair when she saw his start of rapturous delight as he opened the door of the lady! How her soul had burned in agony when she had seen him rush to meet that woman, with her flushing cheek and sparkling eye of triumph; when she had seen him lead her forth, his whole frame kindled with the joy of recovered life; when she had heard the glad shouts from the multitude, and the wild ringing of the happy bells; when she had seen the priest, with his joyous followers, advance to the couple, and make them man and wife before her very eyes; and when she had seen them walk away together upon their path of flowers, followed by the tremendous shouts of the hilarious multitude, in which her one despairing shriek was lost and drowned!

Would it not be better for him to die at once, and go to wait for her in the blessed regions of semibarbaric futurity?

And yet, that awful tiger, those shrieks, that blood!

Her decision had been indicated in an instant, but it had been made after days and nights of anguished deliberation. She had known she would be asked, she had decided what she would answer, and, without the slightest hesitation, she had moved her hand to the right.

The question of her decision is one not to be lightly considered, and it is not for me to presume to set myself up as the one person able to answer it. And so I leave it with all of you: Which came out of the opened door—the lady, or the tiger?

The Discourager
of Hesitancy

A Continuation of
"The Lady, or the Tiger?"

I T WAS nearly a year after the occurrence of that event in the arena of the semibarbaric king, known as the incident of the lady or the tiger, that there came to the palace of this monarch a deputation of five strangers from a far country. These men, of venerable and dignified aspect and demeanor, were received by a high officer of the court, and to him they made known their errand.

"Most noble officer," said the speaker of the deputation, "it so happened that one of our countrymen was present here, in your capital city, on that momentous occasion when a young man who had dared to aspire to the hand of your king's daughter had been placed in the arena, in the midst of the assembled multitude, and ordered to open one of two doors, not knowing whether a ferocious tiger would spring out upon him, or a beauteous lady would advance, ready to become his bride. Our fellow-citizen who was then present was a man of supersensitive feelings, and at the moment when the youth was about to open the door he was so fearful lest he should behold a horrible spectacle that his nerves failed him, and he fled precipitately from the arena, and, mounting his camel, rode homeward as fast as he could go.

"We were all very much interested in the story which our countryman told us, and we were extremely sorry that he did not wait to see the end of the affair. We hoped, however, that in a few weeks some traveller from your city would come among us and bring us further news, but up to the day when we left our country no such traveller had arrived. At last it was determined that the only thing to be done was to send a deputation to this country, and to ask the question: 'Which came out of the open door, the lady or the tiger?'"

When the high officer had heard the mission of this most respectable deputation, he led the five strangers into an inner room, where they were seated upon soft cushions, and where he ordered coffee, pipes, sherbet, and other semibarbaric refreshments to be served to them. Then, taking his seat before them, he thus addressed the visitors:

"Most noble strangers, before answering the question you have come so far to ask, I will relate to you an incident which occurred not very long after that to which you have referred. It is well known in all regions hereabout that our great king is very fond of the presence of beautiful women about his court. All the ladies in waiting upon the queen and royal family are most lovely maidens, brought here from every part of the kingdom. The fame of this concourse of beauty, unequalled in any other royal court, has spread far and wide, and had it not been for the equally wide-spread fame of the systems of impetuous justice adopted by our king, many foreigners would doubtless have visited our court.

"But not very long ago there arrived here from a distant land a prince of distinguished appearance and undoubted rank. To such a one, of course, a royal audience was granted, and our king met him very graciously, and begged him to make known the object of his visit. Thereupon the prince informed his Royal Highness that, having heard of the superior beauty of the ladies of his court, he had come to ask permission to make one of them his wife.

"When our king heard this bold announcement, his face reddened, he turned uneasily on his throne, and we were all in dread lest some quick words of furious condemnation should leap from out his quivering lips. But by a mighty effort he controlled himself, and after a moment's silence he turned to the prince and said: 'Your request is granted. To-morrow at noon you shall wed one of the fairest damsels of our court.' Then turning to his officers, he said: 'Give orders that everything be prepared for a wedding in this palace at high noon to-morrow. Convey this royal prince to suitable apartments. Send to him tailors, bootmakers, hatters, jewellers, armorers, men of every craft whose services he may need. Whatever he asks, provide. And let all be ready for the ceremony to-morrow.'

" 'But, your Majesty,' exclaimed the prince, 'before we make these preparations, I would like—'

" 'Say no more!' roared the king. 'My royal orders have been given, and nothing more is needed to be said. You asked a boon. I granted it, and I will hear no more on the subject. Farewell, my prince, until to-morrow noon.'

"At this the king arose and left the audience-chamber, while the prince was hurried away to the apartments selected for him. Here came to him tailors, hatters, jewellers, and every one who was needed to fit him out in grand attire for the wedding. But the mind of the prince was much troubled and perplexed.

" 'I do not understand,' he said to his attendants, 'this precipitancy of action. When am I to see the ladies, that I may choose among them? I wish opportunity, not only to gaze upon their forms and faces, but to become acquainted with their relative intellectual development.'

" 'We can tell you nothing,' was the answer. 'What our king thinks right, that will he do. More than this we know not.'

" 'His Majesty's notions seem to be very peculiar,' said the prince, 'and, so far as I can see, they do not at all agree with mine.'

"At that moment an attendant whom the prince had not before noticed came and stood beside him. This was a broad-shouldered man of cheery aspect, who carried, its hilt in his right hand, and its broad back resting on his broad arm, an enormous cimeter, the upturned edge of which was keen and bright as any razor. Holding this formidable weapon as tenderly as though it had been a sleeping infant, this man drew closer to the prince and bowed.

" 'Who are you?' exclaimed his Highness, starting back at the sight of the frightful weapon.

" 'I,' said the other, with a courteous smile, 'am the Discourager of Hesitancy. When our king makes known his wishes to any one, a subject or visitor, whose disposition in some little points may be supposed not wholly to coincide with that of his Majesty, I am appointed to attend him closely, that, should he think of pausing in the path of obedience to the royal will, he may look at me, and proceed.'

"The prince looked at him, and proceeded to be measured for a coat.

"The tailors and shoemakers and hatters worked all night, and the next morning, when everything was ready, and the hour of noon was drawing nigh, the prince again anxiously inquired of his attendants when he might expect to be introduced to the ladies.

" 'The king will attend to that,' they said. 'We know nothing of the matter.'

" 'Your Highness,' said the Discourager of Hesitancy, approaching with a courtly bow, 'will observe the excellent quality of this edge.' And drawing a hair from his head, he dropped it upon the upturned edge of his cimeter, upon which it was cut in two at the moment of touching.

"The prince glanced, and turned upon his heel.

"Now came officers to conduct him to the grand hall of the palace, in which the ceremony was to be performed. Here the prince found the king seated on the throne, with his nobles, his courtiers, and his officers standing about him in magnificent array. The prince was led to a position in front of the king, to whom he made obeisance, and then said:

" 'Your Majesty, before I proceed further—'

"At this moment an attendant, who had approached with a long scarf of delicate silk, wound it about the lower part of the prince's face so quickly and adroitly that he was obliged to cease speaking. Then, with wonderful dexterity, the rest of the scarf was wound around the prince's head, so that he was completely blindfolded. Thereupon the attendant quickly made openings in the scarf over the mouth and ears, so that the prince might breathe and hear,

and fastening the ends of the scarf securely, he re-
tired.

"The first impulse of the prince was to snatch the
silken folds from his head and face, but, as he raised
his hands to do so, he heard beside him the voice of
the Discourager of Hesitancy, who gently whispered: 'I am here, your Highness.' And, with a shud-
der, the arms of the prince fell down by his side.

"Now before him he heard the voice of a priest,
who had begun the marriage service in use in that
semi-barbaric country. At his side he could hear a
delicate rustle, which seemed to proceed from fab-
rics of soft silk. Gently putting forth his hand, he
felt folds of such silk close beside him. Then came
the voice of the priest requesting him to take the
hand of the lady by his side; and reaching forth his
right hand, the prince received within it another
hand, so small, so soft, so delicately fashioned, and
so delightful to the touch, that a thrill went through
his being. Then, as was the custom of the country,
the priest first asked the lady would she have this
man to be her husband; to which the answer gently
came, in the sweetest voice he had ever heard: 'I
will.'

"Then ran raptures rampant through the prince's
blood. The touch, the tone, enchanted him. All the
ladies of that court were beautiful, the Discourager
was behind him, and through his parted scarf he
boldly answered: 'Yes, I will.'

"Whereupon the priest pronounced them man and
wife.

"Now the prince heard a little bustle about him,
the long scarf was rapidly unrolled from his head, and
he turned, with a start, to gaze upon his bride. To
his utter amazement, there was no one there. He

stood alone. Unable on the instant to ask a question or say a word, he gazed blankly about him.

"Then the king arose from his throne, and came down, and took him by the hand.

" 'Where is my wife?' gasped the prince.

" 'She is here,' said the king, leading him to a curtained doorway at the side of the hall.

" 'The curtains were drawn aside, and the prince, entering, found himself in a long apartment, near the opposite wall of which stood a line of forty ladies, all dressed in rich attire, and each one apparently more beautiful than the rest.

"Waving his hand toward the line, the king said to the prince: 'There is your bride! Approach, and lead her forth! But remember this: that if you attempt to take away one of the unmarried damsels of our court, your execution shall be instantaneous. Now, delay no longer. Step up and take your bride.'

"The prince, as in a dream, walked slowly along the line of ladies, and then walked slowly back again. Nothing could he see about any one of them to indicate that she was more of a bride than the others. Their dresses were all similar, they all blushed, they all looked up and then looked down. They all had charming little hands. Not one spoke a word. Not one lifted a finger to make a sign. It was evident that the orders given them had been very strict.

" 'Why this delay?' roared the king. 'If I had been married this day to one so fair as the lady who wedded you, I should not wait one second to claim her.'

"The bewildered prince walked again up and down the line. And this time there was a slight change in the countenances of two of the ladies. One of the fairest gently smiled as he passed her. Another, just as beautiful, slightly frowned.

" 'Now,' said the prince to himself, 'I am sure that it is one of those two ladies whom I have married. But which? One smiled. And would not any woman smile when she saw, in such a case, her husband coming toward her? Then again, on the other hand, would not any woman frown when she saw her husband come toward her and fail to claim her? Would she not knit her lovely brows? Would she not inwardly say, "It is I! Don't you know it? Don't you feel it? Come!" But if this woman had not been married, would she not frown when she saw the man looking at her? Would she not say inwardly, "Don't stop at me! It is the next but one. It is two ladies above. Go on!" Then again, the one who married me did not see my face. Would she not now smile if she thought me comely? But if I wedded the one who frowned, could she restrain her disapprobation if she did not like me? Smiles invite the approach of true love. A frown is a reproach to a tardy advance. A smile—"

" 'Now, hear me!' loudly cried the king. 'In ten seconds, if you do not take the lady we have given you, she who has just been made your bride shall be your widow.'

"And, as the last word was uttered, the Discourager of Hesitancy stepped close behind the prince and whispered: 'I am here!'

"Now the prince could not hesitate an instant; he stepped forward and took one of the two ladies by the hand.

"Loud rang the bells, loud cheered the people, and the king came forward to congratulate the prince. He had taken his lawful bride.

"Now, then," said the high officer to the deputation of five strangers from a far country, "when you can decide among yourselves which lady the prince chose, the one who smiled or the one who frowned, then will I tell you which came out of the open door, the lady or the tiger!"

At the latest accounts the five strangers had not yet decided.

The Griffin
and the Minor Canon

OVER THE great door of an old, old church, which stood in a quiet town of a far-away land, there was carved in stone the figure of a large griffin. The old-time sculptor had done his work with great care, but the image he had made was not a pleasant one to look at. It had a large head, with enormous open mouth and savage teeth. From its back arose great wings, armed with sharp hooks and prongs. It had stout legs in front, with projecting claws, but there were no legs behind, the body running out into a long and powerful tail, finished off at the end with a barbed point. This tail was coiled up under him, the end sticking up just back of his wings.

The sculptor, or the people who had ordered this stone figure, had evidently been very much pleased with it, for little copies of it, also in stone, had been placed here and there along the sides of the church, not very far from the ground, so that people could easily look at them and ponder on their curious forms. There were a great many other sculptures on the outside of this church—saints, martyrs, grotesque heads of men, beasts, and birds, as well as those of other creatures which cannot be named, because nobody knows exactly what they were. But none were so curious and interesting as the great griffin over the door and the little griffins on the sides of the church.

A long, long distance from the town, in the midst of dreadful wilds scarcely known to man, there dwelt the Griffin whose image had been put up over the church door. In some way or other the old-time sculptor had seen him, and afterwards, to the best of his memory, had copied his figure in stone. The Griffin had never known this until, hundreds of years afterwards, he heard from a bird, from a wild animal, or in some manner which it is not easy to find out, that there was a likeness of him on the old church in the distant town.

Now, this Griffin had no idea whatever how he looked. He had never seen a mirror, and the streams where he lived were so turbulent and violent that a quiet piece of water, which would reflect the image of anything looking into it, could not be found. Being, as far as could be ascertained, the very last of his race, he had never seen another griffin. Therefore it was that, when he heard of this stone image of himself, he became very anxious to know what he looked like, and at last he determined to go to the old church and see for himself what manner of being he was. So he started off from the dreadful wilds, and flew on and on until he came to the countries inhabited by men, where his appearance in the air created great consternation. But he alighted nowhere, keeping up a steady flight until he reached the suburbs of the town which had his image on its church. Here, late in the afternoon, he alighted in a green meadow by the side of a brook, and stretched himself on the grass to rest. His great wings were tired, for he had not made such a long flight in a century or more.

The news of his coming spread quickly over the town, and the people, frightened nearly out of their wits by the arrival of so extraordinary a visitor, fled into their houses and shut themselves up. The Griffin called loudly for some one to come to him; but the more he called, the more afraid the people were to show themselves. At length he saw two laborers hurrying to their homes through the fields, and in a terrible voice he commanded them to stop. Not daring to disobey, the men stood, trembling.

"What is the matter with you all?" cried the Griffin. "Is there not a man in your town who is brave enough to speak to me?"

"I think," said one of the laborers, his voice shaking so that his words could hardly be understood, "that—perhaps—the Minor Canon—would come."

"Go, call him, then!" said the Griffin. "I want to see him."

The Minor Canon, who filled a subordinate position in the old church, had just finished the afternoon service, and was coming out of a side door, with three aged women who had formed the weekday congregation. He was a young man of a kind disposition, and very anxious to do good to the people of the town. Apart from his duties in the church, where he conducted services every week-day, he visited the sick and the poor; counselled and assisted persons who were in trouble, and taught a school composed entirely of the bad children in the town, with whom nobody else would have anything to do. Whenever the people wanted something difficult done for them, they always went to the Minor Canon. Thus it was that the laborer thought of the young priest when he found that some one must come and speak to the Griffin.

The Minor Canon had not heard of the strange event, which was known to the whole town except himself and the three old women, and when he was informed of it, and was told that the Griffin had asked to see him, he was greatly amazed and frightened.

"Me!" he exclaimed. "He has never heard of me! What should he want with *me?*"

"Oh, you must go instantly!" cried the two men. "He is very angry now because he has been kept waiting so long, and nobody knows what may happen if you don't hurry to him."

The poor Minor Canon would rather have had his hand cut off than to go out to meet an angry griffin; but he felt that it was his duty to go, for it would be a woeful thing if injury should come to the people of the town because he was not brave enough to obey the summons of the Griffin; so, pale and frightened, he started off.

"Well," said the Griffin, as soon as the young man came near, "I am glad to see that there is some one who has the courage to come to me."

The Minor Canon did not feel very courageous, but he bowed his head.

"Is this the town," said the Griffin, "where there is a church with a likeness of myself over one of the doors?"

The Minor Canon looked at the frightful creature before him, and saw that it was, without doubt, exactly like the stone image on the church. "Yes," he said, "you are right."

"Well, then," said the Griffin, "will you take me to it? I wish very much to see it."

The Minor Canon instantly thought that if the Griffin entered the town without the people knowing what he came for, some of them would probably be frightened to death, and so he sought to gain time to prepare their minds.

"It is growing dark now," he said, very much afraid, as he spoke, that his words might enrage the Griffin, "and objects on the front of the church cannot be seen clearly. It will be better to wait until morning, if you wish to get a good view of the stone image of yourself."

"That will suit me very well," said the Griffin. "I see you are a man of good sense. I am tired, and I will take a nap here on this soft grass, while I cool my tail in the little stream that runs near me. The end of my tail gets red-hot when I am angry or excited, and it is quite warm now. So you may go; but be sure and come early tomorrow morning, and show me the way to the church."

The Minor Canon was glad enough to take his leave, and hurried into the town. In front of the church he found a great many people assembled to hear his report of his interview with the Griffin. When they found that he had not come to spread ruin and devastation, but simply to see his stony likeness on the church, they showed neither relief nor gratification, but began to upbraid the Minor Canon for consenting to conduct the creature into the town.

"What could I do?" cried the young man. "If I should not bring him he would come himself, and perhaps end by setting fire to the town with his red-hot tail."

Still the people were not satisfied, and a great many plans were proposed to prevent the Griffin from coming into the town. Some elderly persons urged that the young men should go out and kill him. But the young men scoffed at such a ridiculous idea. Then some one said that it would be a good thing to destroy the stone image, so that the Griffin would have no excuse for entering the town. This proposal was received with such favor that many of the people ran for hammers, chisels, and crowbars with which to tear down and break up the stone griffin. But the Minor Canon resisted this plan with all the strength of his mind and body. He assured the people that this action would enrage the Griffin beyond measure, for it would be impossible to conceal from him that his image had been destroyed during the night.

But they were so determined to break up the stone griffin that the Minor Canon saw that there was nothing for him to do but to stay there and protect it. All night he walked up and down in front of the church door, keeping away the men who brought ladders by which they might mount to the great stone griffin and knock it to pieces with their hammers and crowbars. After many hours the people were obliged to give up their attempts, and went home to sleep. But the Minor Canon remained at his post till early morning, and then he hurried away to the field where he had left the Griffin.

The monster had just awakened, and rising to his fore legs and shaking himself, he said that he was ready to go into the town. The Minor Canon, therefore, walked back, the Griffin flying slowly through the air at a short distance above the head of his guide. Not a person was to be seen in the streets, and they proceeded directly to the front of the church, where the Minor Canon pointed out the stone griffin.

The real Griffin settled down in the little square before the church and gazed earnestly at his sculptured likeness. For a long time he looked at it. First he put his head on one side, and then he put it on the other. Then he shut his right eye and gazed with his left, after which he shut his left eye and gazed with his right. Then he moved a little to one side and looked at the image, then he moved the other way. After a while he said to the Minor Canon, who had been standing by all this time:

"It is, it must be, an excellent likeness! That breadth between his eyes, that expansive forehead, those massive jaws! I feel that it must resemble me. If there is any fault to find with it, it is that the neck seems a little stiff. But that is nothing. It is an admirable likeness—admirable!"

The Griffin sat looking at his image all the morning and all the afternoon. The Minor Canon had been afraid to go away and leave him, and had hoped all through the day that he would soon be satisfied with his inspection and fly away home. But by evening the poor young man was utterly exhausted, and felt that he must eat and sleep. He frankly admitted this fact to the Griffin, and asked him if he would not like something to eat. He said this because he felt obliged in politeness to do so; but as soon as he had spoken the words, he was seized with dread lest the monster should demand half a dozen babies, or some tempting repast of that kind.

"Oh, no," said the Griffin, "I never eat between the equinoxes. At the vernal and at the autumnal equinox I take a good meal, and that lasts me for half a year. I am extremely regular in my habits, and do not think it healthful to eat at odd times. But if you need food, go and get it, and I will return to the soft grass where I slept last night, and take another nap."

The next day the Griffin came again to the little square before the church, and remained there until evening, steadfastly regarding the stone griffin over the door. The Minor Canon came once or twice to look at him, and the Griffin seemed very glad to see him. But the young clergyman could not stay as he had done before, for he had many duties to perform. Nobody went to the church, but the people came to the Minor Canon's house, and anxiously asked him how long the Griffin was going to stay.

"I do not know," he answered, "but I think he will soon be satisfied with looking at his stone likeness, and then he will go away."

But the Griffin did not go away. Morning after morning he went to the church, but after a time he did not stay there all day. He seemed to have taken a great fancy to the Minor Canon, and followed him about as he pursued his various avocations. He would wait for him at the side door of the church, for the Minor Canon held services every day, morning and evening, though nobody came now. "If any one should come," he said to himself, "I must be found at my post." When the young man came out, the Griffin would accompany him in his visits to the sick and the poor, and would often look into the windows of the school-house where the Minor Canon was teaching his unruly scholars. All the other schools were closed, but the parents of the Minor Canon's scholars forced them to go to school, because they were so bad they could not endure them at home—griffin or no griffin. But it must be said they generally behaved very well when that great monster sat up on his tail and looked in at the school-room window.

When it was perceived that the Griffin showed no sign of going away, all the people who were able to do so, left the town. The canons and the higher officers of the church had fled away during the first day of the Griffin's visit, leaving behind only the Minor Canon and some of the men who opened the doors and swept the church. All the citizens who could afford it shut up their houses and travelled to distant parts, and only the working-people and the poor were left behind. After some days these ventured to go about and attend to their business, for if they did not work they would starve. They were getting a little used to seeing the Griffin, and having been told that he did not eat between equinoxes, they did not feel so much afraid of him as before.

Day by day the Griffin became more and more attached to the Minor Canon. He kept near him a great part of the time, and often spent the night in front of the little house where the young clergyman lived alone. This strange companionship was often burdensome to the Minor Canon. But, on the other hand, he could not deny that he derived a great deal of benefit and instruction from it. The Griffin had lived for hundreds of years, and had seen much, and he told the Minor Canon many wonderful things.

"It is like reading an old book," said the young clergyman to himself. "But how many books I would have had to read before I would have found out what the Griffin has told me about the earth, the air, the water, about minerals, and metals, and growing things, and all the wonders of the world!"

Thus the summer went on, and drew toward its

close. And now the people of the town began to be very much troubled again.

"It will not be long," they said, "before the autumnal equinox is here, and then that monster will want to eat. He will be dreadfully hungry, for he has taken so much exercise since his last meal. He will devour our children. Without doubt, he will eat them all. What is to be done?"

To this question no one could give an answer, but all agreed that the Griffin must not be allowed to remain until the approaching equinox. After talking over the matter a great deal, a crowd of the people went to the Minor Canon, at a time when the Griffin was not with him.

"It is your fault," they said, "that the monster is among us. You brought him here, and you ought to see that he goes away. It is only on your account that he stays here at all, for, although he visits his image every day, he is with you the greater part of the time. If you were not here he would not stay. It is your duty to go away, and then he will follow you, and we shall be free from the dreadful danger which hangs over us."

"Go away!" cried the Minor Canon, greatly grieved at being spoken to in such a way. "Where shall I go? If I go to some other town, shall I not take this trouble there? Have I a right to do that?"

"No," said the people, "you must not go to any other town. There is no town far enough away. You must go to the dreadful wilds where the Griffin lives, and then he will follow you and stay there."

They did not say whether or not they expected the Minor Canon to stay there also, and he did not ask them anything about it. He bowed his head, and went into his house to think. The more he thought, the more clear it became to his mind that it was his duty to go away, and thus free the town from the presence of the Griffin.

That evening he packed a leather bag full of bread and meat, and early the next morning he set out on his journey to the dreadful wilds. It was a long, weary, and doleful journey, especially after he had gone beyond the habitations of men; but the Minor Canon kept on bravely, and never faltered. The way was longer than he had expected, and his provisions soon grew so scanty that he was obliged to eat but a little every day; but he kept up his courage, and pressed on, and after many days of toilsome travel he reached the dreadful wilds.

When the Griffin found that the Minor Canon had left the town, he seemed sorry, but showed no disposition to go and look for him. After a few days had passed, he became much annoyed, and asked some of the people where the Minor Canon had gone. But although the citizens had been so anxious that the young clergyman should go to the dreadful wilds, thinking that the Griffin would immediately follow him, they were now afraid to mention the Minor Canon's destination, for the monster seemed angry already, and if he should suspect their trick, he would doubtless become very much enraged. So every one said he did not know, and the Griffin wandered about disconsolate. One morning he looked into the Minor Canon's school-house, which was always empty now, and thought that it was a shame that everything should suffer on account of the young man's absence.

"It does not matter so much about the church," he said, "for nobody went there. But it is a pity about the school. I think I will teach it myself until he returns."

It was the hour for opening the school, and the

Griffin went inside and pulled the rope which rang the school bell. Some of the children who heard the bell ran in to see what was the matter, supposing it to be a joke of one of their companions. But when they saw the Griffin they stood astonished and scared.

"Go tell the other scholars," said the monster, "that school is about to open, and that if they are not all here in ten minutes I shall come after them."

In seven minutes every scholar was in place.

Never was seen such an orderly school. Not a boy or girl moved or uttered a whisper. The Griffin climbed into the master's seat, his wide wings spread on each side of him, because he could not lean back in his chair while they stuck out behind, and his great tail coiled around in front of the desk, the barbed end sticking up, ready to tap any boy or girl who might misbehave. The Griffin now addressed the scholars, telling them that he intended to teach them while their master was away. In speaking he endeavored to imitate, as far as possible, the mild and gentle tones of the Minor Canon, but it must be admitted that in this he was not very successful. He had paid a good deal of attention to the studies of the school, and he determined not to attempt to teach them anything new, but to review them in what they had been studying. So he called up the various classes, and questioned them upon their previous lessons. The children racked their brains to remember what they had learned. They were so afraid of the Griffin's displeasure that they recited as they had never recited before. One of the boys, far down in his class, answered so well that the Griffin was astonished.

"I should think you would be at the head," said

he. "I am sure you have never been in the habit of reciting so well. Why is this?"

"Because I did not choose to take the trouble," said the boy, trembling in his boots. He felt obliged to speak the truth, for all the children thought that the great eyes of the Griffin could see right through them, and that he would know when they told a falsehood.

"You ought to be ashamed of yourself," said the Griffin. "Go down to the very tail of the class, and if you are not at the head in two days, I shall know the reason why."

The next afternoon this boy was number one.

It was astonishing how much these children now learned of what they had been studying. It was as if they had been educated over again. The Griffin used no severity toward them, but there was a look about him which made them unwilling to go to bed until they were sure they knew their lessons for the next day.

The Griffin now thought that he ought to visit the sick and the poor, and he began to go about the town for this purpose. The effect upon the sick was miraculous. All, except those who were very ill indeed, jumped from their beds when they heard he was coming, and declared themselves quite well. To those who could not get up he gave herbs and roots, which none of them had ever before thought of as medicines, but which the Griffin had seen used in various parts of the world, and most of them recovered. But, for all that, they afterwards said that no matter what happened to them, they hoped that they should never again have such a doctor coming to their bedsides, feeling their pulses and looking at their tongues.

As for the poor, they seemed to have utterly disappeared. All those who had depended upon charity for their daily bread were now at work in some way or other, many of them offering to do odd jobs for their neighbors just for the sake of their meals—a thing which before had been seldom heard of in the town. The Griffin could find no one who needed his assistance.

The summer now passed, and the autumnal equinox was rapidly approaching. The citizens were in a state of great alarm and anxiety. The Griffin showed no signs of going away, but seemed to have settled himself permanently among them. In a short time the day for his semi-annual meal would arrive, and then what would happen? The monster would certainly be very hungry, and would devour all their children.

Now they greatly regretted and lamented that they had sent away the Minor Canon. He was the only one on whom they could have depended in this trouble, for he could talk freely with the Griffin, and so find out what could be done. But it would not do to be inactive. Some step must be taken immediately. A meeting of the citizens was called, and two old men were appointed to go and talk to the Griffin. They were instructed to offer to prepare a splendid dinner for him on equinox day—one which would entirely satisfy his hunger. They would offer him the fattest mutton, the most tender beef, fish and game of various sorts, and anything of the kind he might fancy. If none of these suited, they were to mention that there was an orphan asylum in the next town.

"Anything would be better," said the citizens, "than to have our dear children devoured."

The old men went to the Griffin, but their propositions were not received with favor.

"From what I have seen of the people of this town," said the monster, "I do not think I could relish anything which was prepared by them. They appear to be all cowards, and, therefore, mean and selfish. As for eating one of them, old or young, I could not think of it for a moment. In fact, there was only one creature in the whole place for whom I could have had an appetite, and that is the Minor Canon, who has gone away. He was brave, and good, and honest, and I think I should have relished him."

"Ah!" said one of the old men, very politely, "in that case I wish we had not sent him to the dreadful wilds!"

"What!" cried the Griffin. "What do you mean? Explain instantly what you are talking about!"

The old man, terribly frightened at what he had said, was obliged to tell how the Minor Canon had been sent away by the people, in the hope that the Griffin might be induced to follow him.

When the monster heard this he became furiously angry. He dashed away from the old men and, spreading his wings, flew backward and forward over the town. He was so much excited that his tail became red-hot, and glowed like a meteor against the evening sky. When at last he settled down in the little field where he usually rested, and thrust his tail into the brook, the steam arose like a cloud, and the water of the stream ran hot through the town. The citizens were greatly frightened, and bitterly blamed the old man for telling about the Minor Canon.

"It is plain," they said, "that the Griffin intended at last to go and look for him, and we should have been saved. Now who can tell what misery you have brought upon us?"

The Griffin did not remain long in the little field.

As soon as his tail was cool he flew to the town hall and rang the bell. The citizens knew that they were expected to come there, and although they were afraid to go, they were still more afraid to stay away, and they crowded into the hall. The Griffin was on the platform at one end, flapping his wings and walking up and down, and the end of his tail was still so warm that it slightly scorched the boards as he dragged it after him.

When everybody who was able to come was there, the Griffin stood still and addressed the meeting.

"I have had a contemptible opinion of you," he said, "ever since I discovered what cowards you are, but I had no idea that you were so ungrateful, self-ish, and cruel as I now find you to be. Here was your Minor Canon, who labored day and night for your good, and thought of nothing else but how he might benefit you and make you happy; and as soon as you imagine yourselves threatened with a danger,—for well I know you are dreadfully afraid of me,—you send him off, caring not whether he returns or per-ishes, hoping thereby to save yourselves. Now, I had conceived a great liking for that young man, and had intended, in a day or two, to go and look him up. But I have changed my mind about him. I shall go and find him, but I shall send him back here to live among you, and I intend that he shall enjoy the reward of his labor and his sacrifices. Go, some of you, to the officers of the church, who so cowardly ran away when I first came here, and tell them never to return to this town under penalty of death. And if, when your Minor Canon comes back to you, you do not bow yourselves before him, put him in the highest place among you, and serve and honor him all his life, beware of my terrible vengeance! There were only two good things in this town: the Minor

Canon and the stone image of myself over your church door. One of these you have sent away, and the other I shall carry away myself."

With these words he dismissed the meeting; and it was time, for the end of his tail had become so hot that there was danger of its setting fire to the building.

The next morning the Griffin came to the church, and tearing the stone image of himself from its fastenings over the great door, he grasped it with his powerful fore-legs and flew up into the air. Then, after hovering over the town for a moment, he gave his tail an angry shake, and took up his flight to the dreadful wilds. When he reached this desolate region, he set the stone griffin upon a ledge of a rock which rose in front of the dismal cave he called his home. There the image occupied a position somewhat similar to that it had had over the church door; and the Griffin, panting with the exertion of carrying such an enormous load to so great a distance, lay down upon the ground, and regarded it with much satisfaction. When he felt somewhat rested he went to look for the Minor Canon. He found the young man, weak and half starved, lying under the shadow of a rock. After picking him up and carrying him to his cave, the Griffin flew away to a distant marsh, where he procured some roots and herbs which he well knew were strengthening and beneficial to man, though he had never tasted them himself. After eating these the Minor Canon was greatly revived, and sat up and listened while the Griffin told him what had happened in the town.

"Do you know," said the monster, when he had finished, "that I have had, and still have, a great liking for you?"

"I am very glad to hear it," said the Minor Canon, with his usual politeness.

"I am not at all sure that you would be," said the Griffin, "if you thoroughly understood the state of the case, but we will not consider that now. If some things were different, other things would be otherwise. I have been so enraged by discovering the manner in which you have been treated that I have determined that you shall at last enjoy the rewards and honors to which you are entitled. Lie down and have a good sleep, and then I will take you back to the town."

As he heard these words, a look of trouble came over the young man's face.

"You need not give yourself any anxiety," said the Griffin, "about my return to the town. I shall not remain there. Now that I have that admirable likeness of myself in front of my cave, where I can sit at my leisure and gaze upon its noble features and magnificent proportions, I have no wish to see that abode of cowardly and selfish people."

The Minor Canon, relieved from his fears, lay back, and dropped into a doze; and when he was sound asleep, the Griffin took him up and carried him back to the town. He arrived just before daybreak, and putting the young man gently on the grass in the little field where he himself used to rest, the monster, without having been seen by any of the people, flew back to his home.

When the Minor Canon made his appearance in the morning among the citizens, the enthusiasm and cordiality with which he was received were truly wonderful. He was taken to a house which had been occupied by one of the banished high officers of the place, and every one was anxious to do all that could be done for his health and comfort. The people crowded into the church when he held services, so that the three old women who used to be his week-day congregation could not get to the best seats, which they had always been in the habit of taking; and the parents of the bad children determined to reform them at home, in order that he might be spared the trouble of keeping up his former school. The Minor Canon was appointed to the highest office of the old church, and before he died he became a bishop.

During the first years after his return from the dreadful wilds, the people of the town looked up to him as a man to whom they were bound to do honor and reverence. But they often, also, looked up to the sky to see if there were any signs of the Griffin coming back. However, in course of time they learned to honor and reverence their former Minor Canon without the fear of being punished if they did not do so.

But they need never have been afraid of the Griffin. The autumnal equinox day came round, and the monster ate nothing. If he could not have the Minor Canon, he did not care for anything. So, lying down with his eyes fixed upon the great stone griffin, he gradually declined, and died. It was a good thing for some of the people of the town that they did not know this.

If you should ever visit the old town, you would still see the little griffins on the sides of the church, but the great stone griffin that was over the door is gone.

The Sisters Three
and the Kilmaree

THERE WERE once three sisters, who were nearly grown up. They were of high birth, but had lost their parents, and were now under the charge of a fairy godmother, who had put them on an island in the sea, where they were to live until they were entirely grown up. They lived in a beautiful little palace on this island, and had everything they wanted. One of these sisters was pretty, one was good, and the other had a fine mind. When the Fairy Godmother had settled everything to her satisfaction, she told the sisters to stay on the island and be happy until they were grown up, and then she sailed away in a kilmaree.

A kilmaree is a boat used exclusively by fairies, and is shaped a good deal like a ram's horn, with little windows and doors in various parts of it. The waters between the main-land and the island of the sisters were full of strange, entangled currents, and could be navigated only by a boat like a kilmaree, which could twist about as much as any current or stream of water could possibly twist or turn. Of course these boats are very hard to manage, for the passengers sometimes have to get into one door, and sometimes into another; and the water sometimes comes in at a front window and goes out at a back one, while at other times it comes in at a back window and goes out at a front one; sometimes the boat twists around and around like a screw, while at other times it goes over and over like a wheel, so that it is easy to see that any one not accustomed to managing such boats would have a hard time if he undertook to make a trip in one.

It was not long after the three sisters had been taken to their island that there came riding, on a road that ran along the shore of the main-land, a lonely prince. This young man had met with many troubles, and made rather a specialty of grief. He was traveling about by himself, seeking to soothe his sorrows by foreign sights. It was now near evening, and he began to look for a suitable spot to rest and weep. He had been greatly given to tears, but his physicians had told him that he must weep only three times a day, before meals. He now began to feel hungry, and he therefore knew it was weeping-time. He dismounted and seated himself under a tree, but he had scarcely shed half a dozen tears before his attention was attracted by the dome of a palace on an island in the sea before him. The island was a long way off, and he would not have noticed the palace-dome had it not been gilded by the rays of the setting sun. The Prince immediately called to a passer-by, and told him to summon the Principal Inhabitant of the adjacent village.

When the Principal Inhabitant arrived, the Prince

asked him who lived in that distant palace, the dome of which was gilded by the rays of the setting sun.

"That palace," replied the other, "is the home of three sisters. One is pretty, one is good, and the other has a fine mind. They are put there to stay until they are grown up."

"Indeed!" exclaimed the Prince. "I feel interested in them already. Is there a ferry to the island?"

"A ferry!" cried the Principal Inhabitant. "I should think not! Nobody ever goes there, or comes from there, except the Fairy Godmother, and she sails in a kilmaree."

"Can you furnish me with a boat of that kind?" asked the Prince.

"No, indeed!" said the Principal Inhabitant. "I haven't the least idea where in the world you could find a kilmaree."

"Very well, then, sir," said the Prince, "you may go. I am much obliged to you for coming to me."

"You are very welcome," said the Principal Inhabitant, and he walked away. The Prince then mounted his horse, rode to the village, ate his supper, and went to bed.

The next morning the Prince shed barely three tears before breakfast, in such a hurry was he to ride away and find the kilmaree in which he might sail to the distant isle and the sisters three. Before he started, he went to the place whence he had first seen the dome of the palace gilded by the rays of the setting sun, and there he whittled a large peg, on which he cut his initials. This peg he drove down on the very spot where he had seated himself to cry, that he might know where to start from in order to reach the island. If he began his voyage from any other place, and the evening sun did not happen to be shining, he thought he might miss his destination. He then rode away as fast as he could go, but he met nobody until he came to the outskirts of a little village. Here, in a small workshop by the side of the road, was a young man busily engaged in making wooden piggins.

This person was an expectant heir. Among the things he expected to inherit were a large fortune from an uncle, a flourishing business from his brother-in-law, a house and grounds from his maternal grandfather, a very valuable machine for peeling currants, from a connection by marriage, and a string of camels from an aged relative. If he inherited any one of these things, he could either live in affluence or start himself in a good business. In the meantime, however, he earned a little money by making piggins. The Prince dismounted, and approached this young man.

"Can you tell me," he said, "if any one in these parts has a kilmaree?"

"I don't so much as know," said the Expectant Heir, sitting down on his work-bench, "what a kilmaree is."

The Prince then told him all he had heard about the kilmaree, and why it was necessary for him to have one to reach the distant isle.

"I expect," said the other, "to inherit a house and grounds. Among the valuable things there I shall find, no doubt, a kilmaree, which I shall be very glad to lend to you; but, perhaps, you will not be willing to wait so long, for the person from whom I am to inherit the house is not yet dead."

"No," said the Prince, "I can not wait at all. I want a kilmaree immediately. Could you not make me one? You seem to work very well in wood."

"I have no doubt I could make one," said the Expectant Heir, "if I only had a model. From what you say, a kilmaree must be of a very peculiar shape, and I would not know how to set about making one. But I know a person who probably understands all about kilmarees. His name is Terzan, and he lives at the other end of this village. Shall we go to him?"

The Prince agreed, and the two then proceeded to the house of Terzan. This individual was a poor young man who lived in a cottage with his mother and five sisters. He had always been considered very smart, and now, though quite young, was the head of the family. He had been educated at a large school near by, in which he was the only scholar. There were a great many masters and professors, and there used to be a great many scholars, but these had all finished their education and had gone away. For a long time there had been no children in that part of the country to take their places. But the masters and teachers hoped their former pupils would marry and settle, and that they would then send their boys and girls to the school. For this reason the school was kept up, for it would be a great pity if there should be no school when the scholars should begin to come in. It was, therefore, with much pleasure that the teachers and masters took Terzan, when a mere boy, into their school. They were afraid they would forget how to teach if they did not have some one to practice on.

Every day Terzan was passed from professor to professor, from teacher to teacher, each one trying to keep him as long as possible, and to teach him as much as he could. When they were not teaching Terzan, the teachers and professors had nothing to do, and time hung heavy on their hands. It is easy to see, therefore, that Terzan was taught most persistently, and, as he was a smart boy, it is probable that he must have learned a good deal. In course of time he was graduated, and although the professors wished him to begin all over again, so as to make himself absolutely perfect in his studies, his family thought it would be much better for him to come home and work for his living. Terzan accordingly went home, and worked in the garden, in order to help support his mother and sisters. These good women, and indeed nearly everybody in the village, thought Terzan was the smartest boy in the world, and that he knew nearly everything that could be learned. After a time, Terzan himself believed that this was partly true, but as he was a boy of sense he never became very vain. He was very fond, however, of having his own way, and if people differed with him he was apt to think that they were ignorant or crack-brained.

The Expectant Heir knew what a clever fellow Terzan was considered to be, and he therefore supposed he knew all about the kilmaree.

But Terzan had never seen such a boat. He knew, however, what a kilmaree was. "It is a vessel that belongs to a fairy," said he, "and it is a curly-kew sort of a thing, which will go through the most twisted currents. If I could see a kilmaree, I could easily make a model of it; and I know where there is one."

"Where? oh, where?" cried the Prince.

"It belongs to a fairy godmother, who lives in a mountain not far from here. It is in a little pond, with a high wall around it. When the moon rises to-night we can go and look at it, and then, when I have carefully considered it, I can make a model of it."

"You need not take that trouble," said the Prince. "You and this young man can just lift the boat out of the pond, and then I can take it and sail away to the distant isle."

"No, indeed!" cried Terzan. "That would be stealing, and we will do nothing of that sort."

"We might borrow it," said the Expectant Heir, "and bring it back again. There could be nothing wrong in that. I have often borrowed things."

But Terzan would listen to neither of these plans; so that night, when the moon rose, they all went to the Fairy's pond, that they might see the kilmaree, and that Terzan might have the opportunity of carefully considering it, so that he could make a model of it. Terzan had a good idea about such things, and he studied and examined the kilmaree until he was perfectly satisfied that he could make one like it. Then they went home, and the next morning work was commenced upon the vessel. The Expectant Heir was used to working in wood, having been a piggin-maker for several years, and he, therefore, was expected to do the actual work on the kilmaree, while Terzan planned it out and directed its construction. The Prince was in a great hurry to have the vessel finished, and said that he hoped that they would work at it night and day until it was done.

"And what are you going to do?" said Terzan.

"I shall wait as patiently as I can until it is finished," said the Prince. "I dare say I can find some way of amusing myself."

"But you expect to sail in it when it is finished?" asked Terzan.

"Of course I do," replied the Prince, proudly. "What do you mean by such a question?"

"Then, if you expect to sail in this kilmaree," said Terzan, "you must just go to work and help build her. If you don't do that, you shall not travel one inch in her. And, as you do not appear to know anything about ship-building, you may carry the boards and boil the pitch."

The Prince did not like this plan at all; but, as he saw very plainly that there was no other chance of his sailing in a kilmaree, he carried the boards and he boiled the pitch. The three worked away very hard for several days, until at last their boat began to look something like a kilmaree.

It must not be supposed that the Fairy was ignorant of what was going on. She had sat and watched the three companions while Terzan examined and studied her kilmaree, and she knew exactly what they intended to do, and why they wished to do it. She knew very well they could never build a vessel of the proper kind, but she let them work on until they had nearly finished their kilmaree. She could see, as well as anybody could see anything, that, if that vessel were ever launched upon the water, it would immediately screw itself, with everybody on board, down to the bottom of the ocean. It was not her intention that anything of this kind should happen, and so, at night, after the three workers had gone to bed, she removed their vessel, and had her own kilmaree put in its place in the work-shop of the Expectant Heir.

In the morning, when the three companions came to put the finishing touches to their work, Terzan began to compliment the Expectant Heir upon the excellent manner in which he had built the vessel.

"You really have made a splendid kilmaree," said he. "I don't believe there is anything more to be done to it."

"It does seem to be all right," said the other, "but I never should have built it so well had you not told me exactly how to do it."

The Prince expected one or the other would say

something about the admirable manner in which he had carried the boards and boiled the pitch; but, as neither of them said anything of the kind, he merely remarked that it was a very good kilmaree, and the sooner it was launched the better. To this the others agreed, and the same day the vessel was carried down to the shore and placed in the water.

"Now, then," said the Prince, when this had been done, "I shall sail along the coast until I reach the spot where I drove my peg, and then I shall go directly across to the distant isle. I am very much obliged to both of you for what you have done, and when I come back I will pay you something for your trouble."

"Then," asked Terzan, "you expect to sail alone in this kilmaree?"

"Oh, yes," replied the Prince. "I know the direction in which to steer it, and there is no necessity for any one coming with me."

"Indeed!" cried Terzan. "Do you suppose we built this boat just for you to sail to the distant isle? I never heard such nonsense. We, too, are going to sail in this kilmaree, and, as you were good enough to carry the boards and boil the pitch, we will take you with us, if you behave yourself. So, if you want to go, just jump aboard, and clap your hand over the forward spout-hole. It will be your duty to keep that shut, except when I tell you to leave it open. And you," said he to the Expectant Heir, "may sit in the middle, and open and shut the little door on the right where the water runs in, and open and shut the little door on the left where it runs out. I'll steer. All aboard!"

There was nothing else for the Prince to do, and so he jumped on the kilmaree, and clapped his hand over the forward spout-hole. The Expectant Heir went to his duties in the middle of the vessel. And Terzan sat in the stern to steer. But he did not steer at all. The Fairy was there, although he did not see her, and she made the kilmaree go just where she pleased.

Off they started, and very soon the three companions found that sailing in a kilmaree was no great fun. Just to amuse herself, the Fairy made it twist and turn and bob up and down in the water in the most astonishing manner. Several times, when the boat rolled over, the Prince tumbled overboard, and then the kilmaree dipped down and scooped him up, making the others just as wet as he was. The Expectant Heir, at his post in the middle of the vessel, found the waters sometimes rush in so fast at one little door, and rush out so fast at the other, that he thought it would wash all the color out of him. Sometimes the kilmaree would stand up on one end and then bore itself far down into the water, rubbing against sharks and great, fat turtles, and darting about as if it were chasing the smaller fish; then, just as Terzan and his companions feared they were going to be drowned, it would come to the surface and begin to squirm along on top of the water. The others thought that Terzan did not know how to steer, and he admitted that perhaps he did not guide the kilmaree in exactly the proper way, but he hoped that after some practice he would become more skillful.

It began to be dark; but, as there was no stopping the kilmaree, which sailed by some inward power of its own, they were obliged to keep on. Terzan thought he could steer by the stars, and so they all tried to be as well satisfied as possible. But the Fairy knew very well how to steer, and as soon as it became dark she steered right away from the distant isle of the sisters three, and sailed toward a large island far out in the ocean. About midnight they arrived there, and the three companions immediately jumped on shore.

"I am glad to be out of that horrible kilmaree!" said the Prince, "but how in the world am I to find the palace and the sisters three? It is as dark as pitch."

"You will have to wait till morning," said Terzan, "when we will go and help you look for it."

"You need not go at all," said the Prince. "I can easily find it when it is light."

"We shall certainly go with you," said Terzan, "for we want to find the palace as much as you do. Don't we?" said he, addressing the Expectant Heir.

"Indeed, we do," replied that individual.

"The palace I am looking for," said the Prince, "is occupied by three sisters of very high degree, and why a poor young gardener and a pigginist should wish to call upon such ladies, I can't, for the life of me, imagine."

"We will show you that when we get there," said Terzan; and he laid himself down on the sand and went to sleep. The two others soon followed his example.

As for the Fairy Godmother, she left the three young men, and went to a castle near by, which was inhabited by an Afrite. This terrible creature had command of the island, which belonged to the Fairy Godmother, and was tenanted by many strange beings. "I have brought you," said she to the Afrite, "three very foolish persons; one of them is a poor young gardener, who thinks he is a great deal better off than he is; one of them is an expectant heir, who expects to be much better off than he ever will be; and the other is a Prince, who does not know how well off he is. What I want you to do with these three persons, who are all very young men, is to take the nonsense out of them."

"I'll undertake the task with pleasure," said the Afrite, with what was intended to be a bland and re-assuring smile.

"Very well," said the Fairy, "and when the nonsense is entirely out of them, you can hoist a copper-colored flag on the topmost pinnacle of your castle, and I will come over and take charge of them."

And then she left the castle, and sailed away in her kilmaree.

The next morning, when the three young men awoke, they saw the great black Afrite sitting on the sand before them. Frightened and astonished, they sprang to their feet. The Prince first found courage to speak.

"Is this the island of the sisters three?" he asked.

"No," replied the Afrite, with an unpleasant grin; "it is my island. There are plenty of sisters here, and brothers, too; but we don't divide them up into threes."

"Then we have made a mistake," said Terzan. "Let us go back. Where is our kilmaree?"

"Your kilmaree is not here," said the Afrite, sternly, rising to his feet; "you haven't any, and you never had one. The thing you made would not work, and the Fairy Godmother brought you here in her own kilmaree."

The three companions looked at each other in astonishment.

"Yes," continued the Afrite, "she sat in her little cranny in the stern, and steered you to this island. She has told me all about you. You are three young men who don't know how to take care of your-selves. How did you ever dare to think of going to

49

the island of the sisters three, and of stealing the model of the Fairy's kilmaree?"

"I wanted to see the beautiful palace and the three sisters," said the Prince. "It seemed a novel and a pleasant thing to do."

"That was my case also," said Terzan.

"And mine," said the Expectant Heir.

"And so, just to please yourselves," said the Afrite, "you were going to a place where you knew you were not wanted, and where, by going, you would interfere with kind and beneficent plans. You need say no more. You are not fit to take care of yourselves, and what you need is a guardian apiece. Come along, that I may put you under their care."

The three young men mournfully followed the Afrite to his castle. He led them through its gloomy halls to a great court-yard in its center. This yard was filled with all sorts of unnatural creatures. Here were two or three great, grim giants chained together; here and there sat a sulky-looking genie surrounded by mischievous elves and fairies, while, scattered about, were gnomes, and dwarfs, and imps, and many other creatures which our friends had never seen nor heard of. The island seemed a sort of penal colony for such beings, every one of whom looked as if he or she had been sent there for some offense.

"Now, then," said the Afrite to the young men, "I will give you the privilege of choosing your own guardians. Go into that yard, and each pick out the one you would like to have take care of you."

The young men did not want to have anything to do with these strange beings, but there was no disobeying the Afrite. So they went into the court-yard and looked about them. In a short time each had selected a guardian. The Prince chose a malignant fay. The Afrite told him what she was, but the Prince said she was such a little thing, and had such a pleasing aspect, that he would prefer her to any of the others. So the Afrite let him take her. The Expectant Heir selected a spook, and Terzan chose a dryad.

"Now, then," said the Afrite, "begone! And I hope it will not be long before I have a good report of you."

The Malignant Fay led the Prince to the seashore. As he walked along he remembered that for several days he had forgotten to weep before meals. The sisters three and the kilmaree had entirely filled his mind. So he wept copiously to make up for lost time.

"Now, then," said the Fay, with a smile, "sit down on the sand and tell me all about yourself. How do you live when you are at home?"

Then the Prince sat down and told her all about the beautiful palace, the fine kingdom, and the loving subjects he had left in order to find something novel and pleasant that would make him forget his grief.

"What is it you would like more than anything else?" she asked.

"I think I would rather go to the isle of the sisters three than to do anything else," he said.

"All right!" said the Malignant Fay. "You shall go there. Pick up that ax and that bag of nails you see lying there, and follow me into the forest."

The Prince picked up the ax and the nails, and followed his guardian. When, after a long and toilsome walk, he reached the center of the forest, the Malignant Fay pointed out to him an enormous tree.

"Cut down that tree," she said. "And when that is done you shall split it up into boards and planks, and then you shall build a boat in which to sail to the distant isle of the sisters three. While you are working, I will curl myself up in the heart of this lily and take a nap."

The poor Prince had never used an ax in his life, but he felt that he must obey his guardian. And so he began to chop the tree. But he soon became very tired, and sat down to rest. Instantly the Fay sprang from her lily, and pricked him in the face with a sharp bodkin. Howling with pain, the Prince seized his ax, and began to work again.

"There must be no stopping and resting," cried his guardian. "You must work all day, or the boat will never be built."

And so the Prince worked all day, and for many, many days. At nightfall, his guardian allowed him to stop and pick some berries for his supper. And then he slept upon the ground. He now not only wept before each meal, but he shed a tear before each berry that he ate.

As the Expectant Heir and his guardian left the castle, the Afrite beckoned the Spook to one side, and said:

"Do you think you can manage him?"

The Spook made no answer, but opening his eyes until they were as wide as tea-cups, he made them revolve with great rapidity. He then grinned until his mouth stretched all around his head, and his lips met behind his ears. Then he lifted his right leg, and wound it several times around his neck; after which he winked with his left ear. This is a thing which no one but a spook can do.

The Afrite smiled. "You'll do it," said he.

"Now, then," said the Spook to the Expectant Heir, after they had gone some distance from the

castle, "I am famishing for exercise. Will you hold
this stick out at arm's length?"

The Expectant Heir took a stick about a yard long,
which the Spook handed him, and he held it out
horizontally at arm's length. The Spook then stood
on tiptoe, and stuck the other end of the stick into
the middle of his back. He was a smoky, vapory sort
of being, and it did not seem to make any difference
to him whether a stick was stuck into him or not.
Throwing out his legs and arms, he began to revolve
with great rapidity around the stick. He went so fast
he looked like an enormous pinwheel, and, as his
weight was scarcely anything at all, the Expectant
Heir held him out without difficulty. Soon he began
to go so fast that, one after another, his arms, legs,
and head flew off, and fell to the ground at some
distance. Then the body stopped whirling.

"Hello!" said the head. "Will you please pick me
up, and put me together?"

So the Expectant Heir gathered up the arms, legs,
and head. "I hope," said he, "that I shall be able to
stick you together properly."

"Oh, it doesn't matter much," said the Spook,
whose head was now on his body. "Sometimes I
have a leg where an arm ought to be, and sometimes
an arm in a leg's place. I don't really need arms and
legs. I wear them only because it is the fashion.
Come along!"

They then proceeded up a steep and stony hill,
and paused under a tall tree with a few branches
near the top. The Spook languidly clambered up the
trunk of this tree, and hitched his right foot to the
end of one of the limbs. Then, hanging head down-
ward, he slowly descended, his legs stretching out
as he gradually approached the ground. When his
head was opposite that of the Expectant Heir, he

turned up his face and gazed steadily at him, revolving his eyes as he did so. Had the Expectant Heir been a little boy, he would have been very much frightened.

"What do you want most in this world?" asked the Spook.

"A large fortune, a flourishing business, a house and grounds, a machine for peeling currants, and a string of camels," answered the Expectant Heir.

"Do you want them all, or would two or three of them do?" asked the other.

"Two or three would do very well, but I would not object to have them all."

"Would you like to have them now?" asked the Spook, "or are you disposed to postpone the fulfillment of your wishes until some indefinite period, when you may actually come into possession of what you desire?"

"Wait till I get them, you mean?" said the Expectant Heir.

"Precisely," answered the other.

"I have been doing that for a long time," said the Expectant Heir, rather pensively.

"Indeed!" observed the Spook; and turning away his head, he began to try to unhitch his foot from the limb. Finding he could not do this, he climbed up his leg, hand over hand, and unfastened his foot. Then he dropped to the ground, and, drawing his leg in to its ordinary size, he started off again up the hill, the Expectant Heir closely following. When they reached the top of the hill, the Spook stopped before five small trees which grew close together in a row.

"I want you to stay here and watch these trees," said the Spook to the Expectant Heir. "One of them bears plums, another peaches, another dates, another pomegranates, and the last one bears watermelons."

"Watermelons don't grow on trees!" cried the Expectant Heir.

"There is no knowing where they will grow," said the Spook. "You can't be sure that they will never grow on trees until you see they don't. You must watch these trees until they have each borne ripe fruit. There are no buds yet, but they will soon come; then the blossoms will appear; and then the green fruit; and after a while, in the course of time, the fruit will ripen. Then you will have something to eat."

"Oh, I can't wait so long as that!" cried the Expectant Heir. "I am hungry now."

"You can wait easily enough," said the Spook; "you are used to it. Now, stand under these trees and do as I tell you. I will bring you something now and then to take off the edge of your appetite."

So the Expectant Heir stood and watched, and watched. It was weary work, for the buds swelled very slowly, and he did not know when the blossoms would come out.

One day, the Spook came to him and asked: "Do you like pickled lemons?"

"They must be dreadfully sour," said the Expectant Heir, screwing up his face at the thought.

"That is all I have got for you to-day," said the Spook, "therefore you'll have to eat them or go hungry."

So he had to eat the pickled lemons, for he was very hungry.

Another day, the Spook said: "Would you like some peppered peppers?"

"Peppered peppers!" exclaimed the Expectant Heir in horror.

"They are red peppers stuffed with black pepper," said the Spook. "I expect they are hot, but you'll have to eat them, for they are all I have got."

So the Expectant Heir had to eat the peppered peppers, for the fruit-trees had barely begun to blossom.

"Would you like some ice-cream?" the Spook said, another time. "I've only the kind which is flavored with mustard and onion-juice, but you'll have to eat it, for it is all I have got."

Day after day the Spook brought such disagreeable food to the Expectant Heir, who was obliged to eat it, for these fruit-trees were just as slow as any other trees in bringing forth their fruit, and the poor young man could not starve to death.

The Afrite told the Dryad to take Terzan and be a guardian to him. "You can take him about all day," he said, "but at night you must go to your tree and be shut up."

As they went out of the castle, the Dryad explained to Terzan that she had been sent to that island as a punishment for abandoning the tree she should have inhabited. "I now spend the days in this castle," she said, "and the nights in a tree over there in the forest. I am glad to get out. Come along, and I will show you something worth seeing."

As they went along, they passed a little garden in which some gnomes were working, and Terzan stopped to look at them.

"What do you see there?" asked the Dryad, impatiently.

"Oh, I take great interest in such things," replied Terzan. "I have a little garden myself, and it is one of the best in all the country round. When I am at home, I work in it all day."

"I thought you had a good education," said the

Dryad, "and could do better things than to dig and hoe all day."

"I have a good education," said Terzan, "and, what is more, no man can dig potatoes or hoe turnips better than I can."

"Humph!" sneered the Dryad. "A fellow could do those things who had no education at all. I'd as soon be shut up in a tree as to spend my life digging and hoeing, when I knew so much about better things. Come along."

Day after day the Dryad led Terzan to lofty mountaintops, whence he could see beautiful landscapes, with lakes and rivers lying red and golden under the setting sun, and whence he could, sometimes, have glimpses across the waters of distant cities, with their domes and minarets sparkling in the light.

"Do you not think those landscapes are lovely?" said the Dryad. "And there are lovelier views on earth than these. And, if you ever visit those cities, you will find so many wonderful things that it will take all your life to see and understand them."

On other days she took him to the cell of a hermit. The good man was generally absent looking for water-cresses, but his extensive library was always open to the Dryad and her ward. There they sat for hours and hours, reading books which told of the grand and wonderful things that are found in the various parts of the earth.

"Isn't this better than being shut up in a tree, or a little garden?" said the Dryad.

"Perhaps it is," said Terzan, "but my garden was a very good one, and it helped to support my mother and sisters."

"He'll have to see a good many more things," said the Dryad to herself.

All this time the three sisters on the distant isle

had no idea that three young men had ever thought of visiting them in a kilmaree. They lived tranquilly, pursuing their studies, and enjoying the recreations and healthful exercises for which the Fairy Godmother had made the most admirable arrangements. Their palace was furnished with everything they needed, and three happier sisters could nowhere be found.

In the course of time the Afrite went to look into the condition of the young men who had been intrusted to him. He first visited the Prince, and found him still chopping away at his tree.

"How do you feel by this time?" asked the Afrite.

"I feel," said the Prince, leaning wearily upon his ax, for he was not afraid of the Malignant Fay now that the Afrite was by, "that I wish I had never left my kingdom to seek to soothe my sorrows by foreign sights. My troubles there were nothing to what I endure here. In fact, from what I have seen since I left my home, I think they were matters of slight importance, and I am very sure I did not know how well off I was."

"Ha! ha!" said the Afrite, and he walked away. He next went to the hill-top where the Expectant Heir was watching the fruit-trees. "How do you feel now?" said the Afrite to the young man.

"I am sick of expecting things," said he. "If I ever get back to my old home, I am never going to expect any good thing to happen to me unless I can make it happen."

"Then you don't like waiting for this fruit to ripen?" said the Afrite.

"I think it is the most tiresome and disagreeable thing in the world," said the Expectant Heir.

"I thought you were used to expecting things," said the Afrite.

"Oh, I was a fool!" said the other. "I had no right to expect to be as well off as I thought I would be."

Just then the Spook came up with a gruel of brine-water thickened with salt.

"You need not give him that," said the Afrite.

When the Afrite came to the hermit's cell, where he found Terzan and the Dryad, he asked the young man how he felt now.

"I feel," said Terzan, looking up from his book, "as if I had wasted a great deal of valuable time. There are so many wonderful things to be seen and to be done in this world, and I, with a good education, have been content to dig potatoes and hoe turnips in my little garden! It amazes me to think that I should have been satisfied with such a life! I see now that I thought myself a great deal better off than I was."

"Oh, ho!" said the Afrite, and he walked away to his castle, and hoisted a copper-colored flag upon the topmost pinnacle.

The Fairy immediately came over in her kilmaree. "Is the nonsense all out of them?" she said, when she met the Afrite.

"Entirely," he replied.

"All right, then!" she cried. "Dismiss the guardians, and send for the boys."

The three young men were brought to the castle, where they were furnished with a good meal and new clothes. Then they went outside to have a talk with the Fairy.

"I think you are now three pretty sensible fellows," said she. "You, Terzan, have not been punished like the other two, because, although you wasted your time and talents, you worked hard to help support your mother and sisters. But you two never did anything for any one but yourselves, and

I am not sorry that you have had a pretty hard time of it on this island. But that is all over, and, now that the nonsense is entirely out of you all, how would you like to sail in my kilmaree, and visit the isle of the sisters three?"

"We should like it very much, indeed!" they answered all together.

"Then come along!" she said. And they went on board of the kilmaree.

This time the Fairy steered the vessel swiftly and smoothly to the distant isle. The kilmaree turned and screwed about among the twisted currents; but the motion was now so pleasant that the passengers quite liked it. The three young men were taken into a beautiful room in the palace, and there the Fairy made them a little speech.

"I like you very much," she said, "now that the nonsense is out of you; if you don't object, I intend you to marry the sisters three."

"We don't object at all!" they replied.

"Very well," said the Fairy. "And Terzan, I will give you the first choice. Will you take the pretty one? the good one? or the one with a fine mind?"

Terzan really wanted the pretty one, but he thought it was proper to take the one with a fine mind; so he chose her. The Expectant Heir also thought he would like the pretty sister, but, under the circumstances, he thought it would be better for him to take the good one, so he chose her. The pretty one was left for the Prince, who was well satisfied, believing that a lady who would some day be a queen ought to be handsome.

When the sisters came in, and were introduced to their visitors, the three young men were very much astonished. Each of the sisters was pretty, all were good, and each of them had a fine mind.

The Sisters Three and the Kilmaree

"That comes of their all living together in this way," said the Fairy. "I knew it would be so, for good associations are just as powerful as bad ones, and no one of these sisters was either ugly or bad or stupid to begin with." And then she left them to talk together and get acquainted.

In about an hour the Fairy sent for a priest and had the three couples married. After the weddings they all sailed away in the kilmaree, which would accommodate any number of people that the Fairy chose to put into it. The Prince took his bride to his kingdom, where his people received the young couple with great joy. The Expectant Heir took his wife to his native place, where he went into a good business, and soon found himself in comfortable circumstances. Before long his connection by marriage died, and left him the valuable machine for peeling currants, after which he became quite rich and happy.

Terzan and his wife went to a great city, where he studied all sorts of things, wrote books, and delivered lectures. He did a great deal of good, and made much money. He built a comfortable home for his mother and sisters, and lived in a fine mansion with his wife. When his children were old enough, he sent them to the school where he had been educated.

Every year the three friends took a vacation of a month. They all went, with their wives, to the spot on the shore where the Prince had driven down his peg; then the Fairy took them over to the distant isle in her kilmaree. There they spent their vacation in pleasure and delight, and there were never any six persons in the world who had so little nonsense in them.

The Bee-Man of Orn

IN THE ancient country of Orn there lived an old man who was called the Bee-man, because his whole time was spent in the company of bees. He lived in a small hut, which was nothing more than an immense beehive, for these little creatures had built their honeycombs in every corner of the one room it contained,—on the shelves, under the little table, all about the rough bench on which the old man sat, and even about the headboard and along the sides of his low bed. All day the air of the room was thick with buzzing insects, but this did not interfere in any way with the old Bee-man, who walked in among them, ate his meals, and went to sleep without the slightest fear of being stung. He had lived with the bees so long, they had become so accustomed to him, and his skin was so tough and hard, that they no more thought of stinging him than they would of stinging a tree or a stone.

The Bee-Man of Orn

A swarm of bees made their hive in a pocket of his old leather doublet; and when he put on this coat to take one of his long walks in the forest in search of wild bees' nests, he was very glad to have this hive with him, for if he did not find any wild honey, he would put his hand in his pocket and take out a piece of honeycomb for a luncheon. The bees in his pocket worked very industriously, and he was always certain of having something to eat with him wherever he went. He lived principally upon honey; and when he needed bread or meat, he carried some fine combs to a village near by and bartered them for other food.

He was ugly, untidy, shrivelled, and sun-burnt. He was poor, and the bees seemed to be his only friends. But, for all that, he was happy and contented. He had all the honey he wanted, and his bees, whom he considered the best company in the world, were as friendly and sociable as they could be, and seemed to increase in number every day.

One day there stopped at the hut of the Bee-man a Junior Sorcerer. This young person, who was a student of magic, necromancy, and the kindred arts, was much interested in the Bee-man, whom he had frequently noticed in his wanderings, and he considered him an admirable subject for study. He had had a great deal of useful practice in endeavoring to find out, by the various rules and laws of sorcery, exactly why the old Bee-man did not happen to be something that he was not, and why he was what he happened to be. He had studied this matter a long time, and had found out something.

"Do you know," he said, when the Bee-man came out of his hut, "that you have been transformed?"

"What do you mean by that?" said the other, much surprised.

"You have surely heard of animals and human beings who have been magically transformed into different kinds of creatures?"

"Yes, I have heard of these things," said the Beeman. "But what have I been transformed from?"

"That is more than I know," said the Junior Sorcerer. "But one thing is certain—you ought to be changed back. If you will find out what you have been transformed from, I will see that you are made all right again. Nothing would please me better than to attend to such a case."

Then, having a great many things to study and investigate, the Junior Sorcerer went his way.

This information greatly disturbed the mind of the Bee-man. If he had been changed from something else, he ought to be that other thing, whatever it was. He ran after the young man, and overtook him.

"If you know, kind sir," he said, "that I have been transformed, you surely are able to tell me what it is that I was."

"No," said the Junior Sorcerer, "my studies have not proceeded far enough for that. When I become a senior I can tell you all about it. But, in the meantime, it will be well for you to try to discover for yourself your original form, and when you have done that, I will get some of the learned masters of my art to restore you to it. It will be easy enough to do that, but you cannot expect them to take the time and trouble to find out what it was."

With these words, he hurried away, and was soon lost to view.

Greatly disquieted, the Bee-man retraced his steps, and went to his hut. Never before had he heard anything which had so troubled him.

"I wonder what I was transformed from?" he thought, seating himself on his rough bench. "Could it have been a giant, or a powerful prince, or some gorgeous being whom the magicians or the fairies wished to punish? It may be that I was a dog or a horse, or perhaps a fiery dragon or a horrid snake. I hope it was not one of these. But, whatever it was, every one has certainly a right to his original form, and I am resolved to find out mine. I will start early to-morrow morning, and I am sorry now I have not more pockets to my old doublet, so that I might carry more bees and more honey for my journey.

He spent the rest of the day in making a hive of twigs and straw, and when he had transferred to this some honeycombs and a colony of bees which had just swarmed, he rose before sunrise the next day, put on his leather doublet, bound his new hive to his back, and set forth on his quest, the bees who were to accompany him buzzing about him like a cloud.

As the Bee-man passed through the little village the people greatly wondered at his queer appearance, with the hive upon his back. "The Bee-man is going on a long expedition, this time," they said. But no one imagined the strange business on which he was bent. About noon he sat down under a tree, near a beautiful meadow covered with blossoms, and ate a little honey. Then he untied his hive and stretched himself out on the grass to rest. As he gazed upon his bees hovering above him, some going out to the blossoms in the sunshine, and some returning laden with the sweet pollen, he said to himself: "They know just what they have to do, and they do it. But alas for me! I know not what I may have to do. And yet, whatever it may be, I am determined to do it. In some way or other I will find out what was my original form, and then I will have myself changed back to it."

And now the thought again came to him that perhaps his original form might have been something very disagreeable, or even horrid.

"But it does not matter," he said sturdily. "Whatever I was, that shall I be again. It is not right for any one to retain a form which does not properly belong to him. I have no doubt I shall discover my original form in the same way that I find the trees in which the wild bees hive. When I first catch sight of a bee tree I am drawn toward it, I know not how. Something says to me: 'That is what you are looking for.' In the same way I believe that I shall find my original form. When I see it, I shall be drawn toward it. Something will say to me: 'That is it.'"

When the Bee-man had rested he started off again, and in about an hour he entered a fair domain. Around him were beautiful lawns, grand trees, and lovely gardens, while at a little distance stood the stately palace of the Lord of the Domain. Richly dressed people were walking about or sitting in the shade of the trees and arbors, splendidly caparisoned horses were waiting for their riders, and everywhere were seen signs of opulence and gayety.

"I think," said the Bee-man to himself, "that I should like to stop here for a time. If it should happen that I was originally like any of these happy creatures it would please me much."

He untied his hive, and hid it behind some bushes, and taking off his old doublet, laid that beside it. It would not do to have his bees flying about him if he wished to go among the inhabitants of this fair domain.

For two days the Bee-man wandered about the palace and its grounds, avoiding notice as much as possible, but looking at everything. He saw handsome men and lovely ladies, the finest horses, dogs, and cattle that were ever known, beautiful birds in cages, and fishes in crystal globes, and it seemed to him that the best of all living things were here collected.

At the close of the second day the Bee-man said to himself: "There is one being here toward whom I feel very much drawn, and that is the Lord of the Domain. I cannot feel certain that I was once like him, but it would be a very fine thing if it were so; and it seems impossible for me to be drawn toward any other being in the domain when I look upon him, so handsome, rich, and powerful. But I must observe him more closely, and feel more sure of the matter, before applying to the sorcerers to change me back into a lord of a fair domain."

The next morning the Bee-man saw the Lord of the Domain walking in his gardens. He slipped along the shady paths, and followed him so as to observe him closely, and find out if he were really drawn toward this noble and handsome being. The Lord of the Domain walked on for some time, not noticing that the Bee-man was behind him. But suddenly turning, he saw the little old man.

"What are you doing here, you vile beggar?" he cried, and he gave him a kick that sent him into some bushes that grew by the side of the path.

The Bee-man scrambled to his feet, and ran as fast as he could to the place where he had hidden his hive and his old doublet.

"If I am certain of anything," he thought, "it is that I was never a person who would kick a poor old man. I shall leave this place. I was transformed from nothing that I see here."

He now travelled for a day or two longer, and then he came to a great black mountain, near the bottom of which was an opening like the mouth of a cave.

This mountain, he had heard, was filled with caverns and underground passages, which were the abodes of dragons, evil spirits, and horrid creatures of all kinds.

"Ah me!" said the Bee-man, with a sigh, "I suppose I ought to visit this place. If I am going to do this thing properly, I should look on all sides of the subject, and I may have been one of those dreadful creatures myself."

Thereupon he went to the mountain, and as he approached the opening of the passage which led into its inmost recesses, he saw, sitting upon the ground, and leaning his back against a tree, a Languid Youth.

"Good day," said this individual, when he saw the Bee-man. "Are you going inside?"

"Yes," said the Bee-man, "that is what I intend to do."

"Then," said the Languid Youth, slowly rising to his feet, "I think I will go with you. I was told that if I went in there I should get my energies toned up, and they need it very much. But I did not feel equal to entering by myself, and I thought I would wait until some one came who was going in. I am very glad to see you, and we will enter together."

So the two went into the cave, and they had proceeded but a short distance when they met a very little creature, whom it was easy to recognize as a Very Imp. He was about two feet high, and resembled in color a freshly polished pair of boots. He was extremely lively and active, and came bounding toward them.

"What did you two people come here for?" he asked.

"I came," said the Languid Youth, "to have my energies toned up."

"You have come to the right place," said the Very Imp. "We will tone you up. And what does that old Bee-man want?"

"He has been transformed from something, and wants to find out what it is. He thinks he may have been one of the things in here."

"I should not wonder if that were so," said the Very Imp, rolling his head on one side and eying the Bee-man with a critical gaze. "All right," continued the Very Imp, "he can go around and pick out his previous existence. We have here all sorts of vile creepers, crawlers, hissers, and snorters. I suppose he thinks anything will be better than a Bee-man."

"It is not because I want to be better than I am," said the Bee-man, "that I started out on this search. I have simply an honest desire to become what I originally was."

"Oh! that is it, is it?" said the other. "There is an idiotic moon-calf here, with a clam head, which must be very much like what you used to be."

"Nonsense," said the Bee-man. "You have not the least idea what an honest purpose is. I shall go about and see for myself."

"Go on," said the Very Imp, "and I will attend to this fellow who wants to be toned up." So saying, he joined the Languid Youth.

"Look here," said that individual, regarding him with interest, "do you black and shine yourself every morning?"

"No," said the other, "it is waterproof varnish. You want to be invigorated, don't you? Well, I will tell you a splendid way to begin. You see that Bee-man has put down his hive and his coat with the bees in it. Just wait till he gets out of sight, and then catch a lot of those bees and squeeze them flat. If you spread them on a sticky rag, and make a plaster, and put it on the small of your back, it will invigorate you like everything, especially if some of the bees are not quite dead."

"Yes," said the Languid Youth, looking at him with his mild eyes, "but if I had energy enough to catch a bee I would be satisfied. Suppose you catch a lot for me."

"The subject is changed," said the Very Imp. "We are now about to visit the spacious chamber of the King of the Snapdragons."

"That is a flower," said the Languid Youth.

"You will find him a gay old blossom," said the other. "When he has chased you round his room, and has blown sparks at you, and has snorted and howled, and cracked his tail, and snapped his jaws like a pair of anvils, your energies will be toned up higher than ever before in your life."

"No doubt of it," said the Languid Youth. "But I think I will begin with something a little milder."

"Well, then," said the other, "there is a flat-tailed Demon of the Gorge in here. He is generally asleep, and, if you say so, you can slip into the farthest corner of his cave, and I'll solder his tail to the opposite wall. Then he will rage and roar, but he can't get at you, for he doesn't reach all the way across his cave; I have measured him. It will tone you up wonderfully to sit there and watch him."

"Very likely," said the Languid Youth. "But I would rather stay outside and let you go up in the corner. The performance in that way will be more interesting to me."

"You are dreadfully hard to please," said the Very Imp. "I have offered them to you loose, and I have offered them fastened to a wall, and now the best thing I can do is to give you a chance at one of them that can't move at all. It is the Ghastly Griffin, and is enchanted. He can't stir so much as the tip of his whiskers for a thousand years. You can go to his cave and examine him just as if he were stuffed, and then you can sit on his back and think how it would be if you should live to be a thousand years old, and he should wake up while you are sitting there. It would be easy to imagine a lot of horrible things he would do to you when you look at his open mouth with its awful fangs, his dreadful claws, and his horrible wings all covered with spikes.''

"I think that might suit me," said the Languid Youth. "I would much rather imagine the exercises of these monsters than to see them really going on."

"Come on, then," said the Very Imp, and he led the way to the cave of the Ghastly Griffin.

The Bee-man went by himself through a great part of the mountain, and looked into many of its gloomy caves and recesses, recoiling in horror from most of the dreadful monsters who met his eyes. While he was wandering about, an awful roar was heard resounding through the passages of the mountain, and soon there came flapping along an enormous dragon, with body black as night, and wings and tail of fiery red. In his great fore-claws he bore a little baby.

"Horrible!" exclaimed the Bee-man. "He is taking that little creature to some place to devour it."

He saw the dragon enter a cave not far away, and following, looked in. The dragon was crouched upon the ground, with the little baby lying before him. It did not seem to be hurt, but was frightened and crying. The monster was looking upon it with delight, as if he intended to make a dainty meal of it as soon as his appetite should be a little stronger.

"It is too bad!" thought the Bee-man. "Somebody

ought to do something." And turning around, he ran away as fast as he could.

He ran through various passages until he came to the spot where he had left his beehive. Picking it up, he hurried back, carrying the hive in his two hands before him. When he reached the cave of the dragon, he looked in and saw the monster still crouched over the weeping child. Without a moment's hesitation, the Bee-man rushed into the cave and threw his hive straight into the face of the dragon. The bees, enraged by the shock, rushed out in an angry crowd, and immediately fell upon the head, mouth, eyes, and nose of the dragon. The great monster, astounded by this sudden attack, and driven almost wild by the numberless stings of the bees, sprang back to the farthest portion of his cave, still followed by his relentless enemies, at whom he flapped wildly with his great wings and struck with his paws. While the dragon was thus engaged with the bees, the Bee-man rushed forward, seized the child, and hurried away. He did not stop to pick up his doublet, but kept on until he reached the entrance of the caves. There he saw the Very Imp hopping along on one leg, and rubbing his back and shoulders with his hands; he stopped to inquire what was the matter, and what had become of the Languid Youth.

"He is no kind of a fellow," said the Very Imp. "He disappointed me dreadfully. I took him up to the Ghastly Griffin, and told him the thing was enchanted, and that he might sit on its back and think about what it could do if it were awake. But when he came near it the wretched creature opened its eyes and raised its head, and then you ought to have seen how mad that simpleton was. He made a dash at me and seized me by the ears. He kicked and beat me till I can scarcely move."

"His energies must have been toned up a good deal," said the Bee-man.

"Toned up! I should say so!" cried the other. "I raised a howl, and a Scissor-jawed Clipper came out of his hole, and got after him. But that lazy fool ran so fast he could not be caught."

The Bee-man now ran on, and soon overtook the Languid Youth.

"You need not be in a hurry now," said the latter, "for the rules of this institution don't allow the creatures inside to come out of this opening, or to hang around it. If they did, they would frighten away visitors. They go in and out of holes in the upper part of the mountain."

The two proceeded on their way.

"What are you going to do with that baby?" said the Languid Youth.

"I shall carry it along with me as I go on with my search," said the Bee-man, "and perhaps I may find its mother. If I do not, I shall give it to somebody in the little village yonder. Anything would be better than leaving it to be devoured by that horrid dragon."

"Let me carry it. I feel quite strong enough now to carry a baby."

"Thank you," said the Bee-man, "but I can take it myself. I like to carry something, and I have now neither my hive nor my doublet."

"It is very well that you had to leave them behind," said the Youth, "for the bees would have stung the baby."

"My bees never sting babies," said the other.

"They probably never had a chance," remarked his companion.

They soon entered the village, and after walking a short distance the Youth exclaimed: "Do you see that woman over there, sitting at the door of her house? She has beautiful hair, and she is tearing it all to pieces. She should not be allowed to do that."

"No," said the Bee-man. "Her friends should tie her hands."

"Perhaps she is the mother of this child," said the Youth, "and if you give it to her she will no longer think of tearing her hair."

"But," said the Bee-man, "you don't really think this is her child?"

"Suppose you go over and see," said the other.

The Bee-man hesitated a moment, and then he walked toward the woman. Hearing him coming, she raised her head, and when she saw the child she rushed toward it, snatched it into her arms, and screaming with joy, she covered it with kisses. Then with happy tears she begged to know the story of the rescue of her child, whom she never expected to see again. She loaded the Bee-man with thanks and blessings; the friends and neighbors gathered around and there was great rejoicing. The mother urged the Bee-man and the Youth to stay with her and rest and refresh themselves, which they were glad to do, as they were tired and hungry.

They remained at the cottage all night, and in the afternoon of the next day the Bee-man said to the Youth: "It may seem an odd thing to you, but never in all my life have I felt myself drawn toward any living being as I am drawn toward this baby. Therefore I believe that I have been transformed from a baby."

"Good!" cried the Youth. "It is my opinion that you have hit the truth. And would you really like to be changed back to your original form?"

"Indeed I would!" said the Bee-man. "I have the strongest yearning to be what I originally was."

The Youth, who had now lost every trace of languid feeling, took a great interest in the matter, and early the next morning started off to inform the Junior Sorcerer that the Bee-man had discovered what he had been transformed from, and desired to be changed back to it.

The Junior Sorcerer and his learned masters were filled with enthusiasm when they heard this report, and they at once set out for the mother's cottage, where, by magic arts, the Bee-man was changed back into a baby. The mother was so grateful for what the Bee-man had done for her that she agreed to take charge of this baby and to bring it up with her own.

"It will be a grand thing for him," said the Junior Sorcerer, "and I am glad I studied his case. He will now have a fresh start in life, and will have a chance to become something better than a miserable old man living in a wretched hut, with no friends or companions but buzzing bees."

The Junior Sorcerer and his masters then returned to their homes, happy in the success of their great performance. And the Youth went back to his home anxious to begin a life of activity and energy.

Years and years afterward, when the Junior Sorcerer had become a Senior and was very old indeed, he passed through the country of Orn, and noticed a small hut about which swarms of bees were flying. He approached it, and looking in at the door, he saw an old man in a leather doublet, sitting at a table, eating honey. By his magic art he knew this was the baby which had been transformed from the Bee-man.

"Upon my word!" exclaimed the Sorcerer, "he has grown into the same thing again!"

Old Pipes
and the Dryad

A MOUNTAIN BROOK ran through a little village. Over the brook there was a narrow bridge, and from the bridge a foot-path led out from the village and up the hillside to the cottage of Old Pipes and his mother. For many, many years, Old Pipes had been employed by the villagers to pipe the cattle down from the hills. Every afternoon, an hour before sunset, he would sit on a rock in front of his cottage and play on his pipes. Then all the flocks and herds that were grazing on the mountains would hear him, wherever they might happen to be, and would come down to the village—the cows by the easiest paths, the sheep by those not quite so easy, and the goats by the steep and rocky ways that were hardest of all.

But now, for a year or more, Old Pipes had not piped the cattle home. It is true that every afternoon he sat upon the rock and played upon his familiar instrument, but the cattle did not hear him. He had grown old, and his breath was feeble. The echoes of his cheerful notes, which used to come from the rocky hill on the other side of the valley, were heard no more, and twenty yards from Old Pipes one could scarcely tell what tune he was playing. He had become somewhat deaf, and did not know that the sound of his pipes was so thin and weak, and that the cattle did not hear him. The cows, the sheep, and the goats came down every afternoon as before, but this was because two boys and a girl were sent up after them. The villagers did not wish the good old man to know that his piping was no longer of any use, so they paid him his little salary every month, and said nothing about the two boys and the girl.

Old Pipes's mother was, of course, a great deal older than he was, and was as deaf as a gate,—posts, latch, hinges, and all,—and she never knew that the sound of her son's pipe did not spread over all the mountain side, and echo back strong and clear from the opposite hills. She was very fond of Old Pipes, and proud of his piping, and as he was so much younger than she was, she never thought of him as being very old. She cooked for him, and made his bed, and mended his clothes, and they lived very comfortably on his little salary.

One afternoon, at the end of the month, when Old Pipes had finished his piping, he took his stout staff and went down the hill to the village to receive the money for his month's work. The path seemed a great deal steeper and more difficult than it used to be, and Old Pipes thought that it must have been washed by the rains and greatly damaged. He remembered it as a path that was quite easy to traverse either up or down. But Old Pipes had been a very active man, and as his mother was so much older than he was, he never thought of himself as aged and infirm.

When the Chief Villager had paid him, and he had talked a little with some of his friends, Old Pipes started to go home. But when he had crossed the bridge over the brook, and gone a short distance up the hillside, he became very tired, and sat down upon a stone. He had not been sitting there half a minute when along came two boys and a girl.

"Children," said Old Pipes, "I'm very tired to-night, and I don't believe I can climb up this steep path to my home. I think I shall have to ask you to help me."

"We will do that," said the boys and the girl, quite cheerfully. Then one boy took him by the right hand, and the other by the left, while the girl pushed him in the back. In this way he went up the hill quite easily, and soon reached his cottage door. Old Pipes gave each of the three children a copper coin, and then they sat down for a few minutes' rest before starting back to the village.

"I'm sorry that I tired you so much," said Old Pipes.

"Oh, that would not have tired us," said one of the boys, "if we had not been so far to-day after the cows, the sheep, and the goats. They rambled high up on the mountain, and we never before had such a time in finding them."

"Had to go after the cows, the sheep, and the goats!" exclaimed Old Pipes. "What do you mean by that?"

The girl, who stood behind the old man, shook her head, put her hand on her mouth, and made all sorts of signs to the boy to stop talking on this subject. But he did not notice her, and promptly answered Old Pipes.

"Why, you see, good sir," said he, "that as the cattle can't hear your pipes now, somebody has to go after them every evening to drive them down from the mountain, and the Chief Villager has hired us three to do it. Generally it is not very hard work, but to-night the cattle had wandered far."

"How long have you been doing this?" asked the old man.

The girl shook her head and clapped her hand on her mouth more vigorously than before, but the boy went on.

"I think it is about a year now," he said, "since the people first felt sure that the cattle could not hear your pipes, and from that time we've been driving them down. But we are rested now, and will go home. Good night, sir."

The three children then went down the hill, the girl scolding the boy all the way home. Old Pipes stood silent a few moments, and then he went into his cottage.

"Mother," he shouted, "did you hear what those children said?"

"Children!" exclaimed the old woman. "I did not hear them. I did not know there were any children here."

Then Old Pipes told his mother, shouting very loudly to make her hear, how the two boys and the girl had helped him up the hill, and what he had heard about his piping and the cattle.

"They can't hear you?" cried his mother. "Why, what's the matter with the cattle?"

"Ah, me!" said Old Pipes. "I don't believe there's anything the matter with the cattle. It must be with me and my pipes that there is something the mat-

er. But one thing is certain: if I do not earn the
wages the Chief Villager pays me, I shall not take
them. I shall go straight down to the village and give
back the money I received to-day."

"Nonsense!" cried his mother. "I'm sure you've
piped as well as you could, and no more can be expected. And what are we to do without the money?"

"I don't know," said Old Pipes. "But I'm going
down to the village to pay it back."

The sun had now set; but the moon was shining
very brightly on the hillside, and Old Pipes could
see his way very well. He did not take the same
path by which he had gone before, but followed another, which led among the trees upon the hillside,
and, though longer, was not so steep.

When he had gone about half-way, the old man
sat down to rest, leaning his back against a great
oak tree. As he did so, he heard a sound like knocking inside the tree, and then a voice distinctly said:
"Let me out! let me out!"

Old Pipes instantly forgot that he was tired, and
sprang to his feet. "This must be a Dryad tree!" he
exclaimed. "If it is, I'll let her out."

Old Pipes had never, to his knowledge, seen a
Dryad tree, but he knew there were such trees on
the hillsides and the mountains, and that Dryads
lived in them. He knew, too, that in the summer-
time, on those days when the moon rose before the
sun went down, a Dryad could come out of her tree
if any one could find the key which locked her in,
and turn it. Old Pipes closely examined the trunk
of the tree, which stood in the full moonlight. "If I
see that key," he said, "I shall surely turn it." Before
long he perceived a piece of bark standing out from
the tree, which appeared to him very much like the
handle of a key. He took hold of it, and found he

could turn it quite around. As he did so, a large part of the side of the tree was pushed open, and a beautiful Dryad stepped quickly out.

For a moment she stood motionless, gazing on the scene before her—the tranquil valley, the hills, the forest, and the mountain-side, all lying in the soft, clear light of the moon. "Oh, lovely! lovely!" she exclaimed. "How long it is since I have seen anything like this!" And then, turning to Old Pipes, she said: "How good of you to let me out! I am so happy and thankful that I must kiss you, you dear old man!" And she threw her arms around the neck of Old Pipes, and kissed him on both cheeks. "You don't know," she then went on to say, "how doleful it is to be shut up so long in a tree. I don't mind it in the winter, for then I am glad to be sheltered, but in summer it is a rueful thing not to be able to see all the beauties of the world. And it's ever so long since I've been let out. People so seldom come this way, and when they do come at the right time they either don't hear me, or they are frightened and run away. But you, you dear old man, you were not frightened, and you looked and looked for the key, and you let me out, and now I shall not have to go back till winter has come and the air grows cold. Oh, it is glorious! What can I do for you to show you how grateful I am?"

"I am very glad," said Old Pipes, "that I let you out, since I see that it makes you so happy. But I must admit that I tried to find the key because I had a great desire to see a Dryad. But if you wish to do something for me, you can, if you happen to be going down toward the village."

"To the village!" exclaimed the Dryad. "I will go anywhere for you, my kind old benefactor."

"Well, then," said Old Pipes, "I wish you would

take this little bag of money to the Chief Villager, and tell him that Old Pipes cannot receive pay for the services which he does not perform. It is now more than a year that I have not been able to make the cattle hear me when I piped to call them home. I did not know this until tonight, but now that I know it I cannot keep the money, and so I send it back." So handing the little bag to the Dryad, he bade her good night, and turned toward his cottage.

"Good night," said the Dryad. "And I thank you over and over and over again, you good old man!"

Old Pipes walked toward his home, very glad to be saved the fatigue of going all the way down to the village and back again. "To be sure," he said to himself, "this path does not seem at all steep, and I can walk along it very easily, but it would have tired me dreadfully to come up all the way from the village, especially as I could not have expected those children to help me again." When he reached home, his mother was surprised to see him returning so soon.

"What!" she exclaimed, "have you already come back? What did the Chief Villager say? Did he take the money?"

Old Pipes was just about to tell her that he had sent the money to the village by a Dryad, when he suddenly reflected that his mother would be sure to disapprove such a proceeding, and so he merely said he had sent it by a person whom he had met.

"And how do you know that the person will ever take it to the Chief Villager?" cried his mother. "You will lose it, and the villagers will never get it. Oh, Pipes! Pipes! when will you be old enough to have ordinary common sense?"

Old Pipes considered that as he was already seventy years of age he could scarcely expect to grow any wiser, but he made no remark on this subject, and saying that he doubted not that the money would go safely to its destination, he sat down to his supper. His mother scolded him roundly, but he did not mind it, and after supper he went out and sat on a rustic chair in front of the cottage to look at the moonlit village, and to wonder whether or not the Chief Villager really received the money. While he was doing these two things, he went fast asleep.

When Old Pipes left the Dryad, she did not go down to the village with the little bag of money. She held it in her hand, and thought about what she had heard.

"This is a good and honest man," she said, "and it is a shame that he should lose this money. He looked as if he needed it, and I don't believe the people in the village will take it from one who has served them so long. Often, when in my tree, have I heard the sweet notes of his pipes. I am going to take the money back to him." She did not start immediately, because there were so many beautiful things to look at. But after a while she went up to the cottage, and finding Old Pipes asleep in his chair, she slipped the little bag into his coat-pocket, and silently sped away.

The next day Old Pipes told his mother that he would go up the mountain and cut some wood. He had a right to get wood from the mountain, but for a long time he had been content to pick up the dead branches which lay about his cottage. To-day, however, he felt so strong and vigorous that he thought he would go and cut some fuel that would be better than this. He worked all the morning, and when he came back he did not feel at all tired, and had a very good appetite for his dinner.

Now, Old Pipes knew a good deal about Dryads, but there was one thing which, although he had heard, he had forgotten. This was that a kiss from a Dryad makes a person ten years younger. The people of the village knew this, and they were very careful not to let any child of ten years or younger go into the woods where the Dryads were supposed to be, for if they should chance to be kissed by one of these tree nymphs, they would be set back so far that they would cease to exist. A story was told in the village that a very bad boy of eleven once ran away into the woods, and had an adventure of this kind, and when his mother found him he was a little baby of one year old. Taking advantage of her opportunity, she brought him up more carefully than she had done before, and he grew to be a very good boy indeed.

Now, Old Pipes had been kissed twice by the Dryad, once on each cheek, and he therefore felt as vigorous and active as when he was a hale man of fifty. His mother noticed how much work he was doing, and told him that he need not try in that way to make up for the loss of his piping wages, for he would only tire himself out, and get sick. But her son answered that he had not felt so well for years, and that he was quite able to work. In the course of the afternoon, Old Pipes, for the first time that day, put his hand in his coat-pocket, and there, to his amazement, he found the little bag of money. "Well, well!" he exclaimed, "I am stupid indeed! I really thought that I had seen a Dryad, but when I sat down by that big oak tree I must have gone to sleep and dreamed it all, and then I came home thinking I had given the money to a Dryad, when it was in my pocket all the time. But the Chief Villager shall have the money. I shall not take it to him to-day, but to-morrow I wish to go to the village to see some of my old friends, and then I shall give up the money."

Toward the close of the afternoon, Old Pipes, as had been his custom for so many years, took his pipes from the shelf on which they lay, and went out to the rock in front of the cottage.

"What are you going to do?" cried his mother. "If you will not consent to be paid, why do you pipe?"

"I am going to pipe for my own pleasure," said her son. "I am used to it, and I do not wish to give it up. It does not matter now whether the cattle hear me or not, and I am sure that my piping will injure no one."

When the good man began to play upon his favorite instrument he was astonished at the sound that came from it. The beautiful notes of the pipes sounded clear and strong down into the valley, and spread over the hills, and up the sides of the mountain beyond, while, after a little interval, an echo came back from the rocky hill on the other side of the valley.

"Ha, ha!" he cried, "what has happened to my pipes? They must have been stopped up of late, but now they are as clear and good as ever."

Again the merry notes went sounding far and wide. The cattle on the mountain heard them, and those that were old enough remembered how these notes had called them from their pastures every evening, and so they started down the mountain-side, the others following.

The merry notes were heard in the village below, and the people were much astonished thereby. "Why, who can be blowing the pipes of Old Pipes?" they said. But as they were all very busy, no one went up to see. One thing, however, was plain enough: the cattle were coming down the mountain. So the two boys and the girl did not have to go after them, and had an hour for play, for which they were very glad.

The next morning Old Pipes started down to the village with his money, and on the way he met the Dryad. "Oh, ho!" he cried, "is that you? Why, I thought my letting you out of the tree was nothing but a dream."

"A dream!" cried the Dryad. "If you only knew how happy you have made me, you would not think it merely a dream. And has it not benefited you? Do you not feel happier? Yesterday I heard you playing beautifully on your pipes."

"Yes, yes," cried he. "I did not understand it before, but I see it all now. I have really grown younger. I thank you, I thank you, good Dryad, from the bottom of my heart. It was the finding of the money in my pocket that made me think it was a dream."

"Oh, I put it in when you were asleep," she said, laughing, "because I thought you ought to keep it. Good-by, kind, honest man. May you live long, and be as happy as I am now."

Old Pipes was greatly delighted when he understood that he was really a younger man. But that made no difference about the money, and he kept on his way to the village. As soon as he reached it, he was eagerly questioned as to who had been playing his pipes the evening before, and when the people heard that it was himself, they were very much surprised. Thereupon Old Pipes told what had happened to him, and then there was greater wonder, with hearty congratulations and handshakes, for Old Pipes was liked by every one. The Chief Villager refused to take his money, and although Old Pipes said he had not earned it, every one present insisted that, as he could now play on his pipes as before, he should lose nothing because, for a time, he was unable to perform his duty.

So Old Pipes was obliged to keep his money, and after an hour or two spent in conversation with his friends, he returned to his cottage.

There was one individual, however, who was not at all pleased with what had happened to Old Pipes. This was an Echo-dwarf who lived on the hills on the other side of the valley, and whose duty it was to echo back the notes of the pipes whenever they could be heard. There were a great many other Echo-dwarfs on these hills, some of whom echoed back the songs of maidens, some the shouts of children, and others the music that was often heard in the village. But there was only one who could send back the strong notes of the pipes of Old Pipes, and this had been his sole duty for many years. But when the old man grew feeble, and the notes of his pipes could not be heard on the opposite hills, this Echo-dwarf had nothing to do, and he spent his time in delightful idleness; and he slept so much and grew so fat that it made his companions laugh to see him walk.

On the afternoon on which, after so long an interval, the sound of the pipes was heard on the echo hills, this dwarf was fast asleep behind a rock. As soon as the first notes reached them, some of his companions ran to wake him. Rolling to his feet, he echoed back the merry tune of Old Pipes. Naturally, he was very much annoyed and indignant at being thus obliged to give up his life of comfortable leisure, and he hoped that this pipe-playing would not occur again.

But the next afternoon he was awake and listening, and, sure enough, at the usual hour along came the notes of the pipes, as clear and strong as they ever had been, and he was obliged to work as long as Old Pipes played. The Echo-dwarf was very angry. He had supposed, of course, that the pipe-playing had ceased forever, and he felt that he had a right to be indignant at being thus deceived. He was so much disturbed that he made up his mind to go and try to find out whether this was to be a temporary matter or not. He had plenty of time, as the pipes were played but once a day, and he set off early in the morning for the hill on which Old Pipes lived. It was hard work for the fat little fellow, and when he had crossed the valley and had gone some distance into the woods on the hillside, he stopped to rest, and in a few minutes the Dryad came tripping along.

"Ho, ho!" exclaimed the dwarf, "what are you doing here? and how did you get out of your tree?"

"Doing!" cried the Dryad. "I am being happy, that's what I'm doing. I was let out of my tree by the good old man who plays the pipes to call the cattle down from the mountain, and it makes me happier to think that I have been of service to him. I gave him two kisses of gratitude, and now he is young enough to play his pipes as well as ever."

The Echo-dwarf stepped forward, his face pale with passion. "Am I to believe," he said, "that you are the cause of this great evil that has come upon me? that you are the wicked creature who has again started this old man upon his career of pipe-playing? What have I ever done to you that you should have condemned me for years and years to echo back the notes of those wretched pipes?"

At this the Dryad laughed loudly.

"What a funny little fellow you are!" she said.

"Any one would think you had been condemned to toil from morning till night, while what you really have to do is merely to imitate for half an hour every day the merry notes of Old Pipes's piping. Fie upon you, Echo-dwarf! You are lazy and selfish, and that is what is the matter with you. Instead of grumbling at being obliged to do a little wholesome work, which is less, I am sure, than that of any other Echo-dwarf upon the rocky hillside, you should rejoice at the good fortune of the old man who has regained so much of his strength and vigor. Go home and learn to be just and generous, and then, perhaps, you may be happy. Good-by."

"Insolent creature!" shouted the dwarf, as he shook his fat little fist at her. "I'll make you suffer for this. You shall find out what it is to heap injury and insult upon one like me, and to snatch from him the repose that he has earned by long years of toil." And shaking his head savagely, he hurried back to the rocky hillside.

Every afternoon the merry notes of the pipes of Old Pipes sounded down into the valley and over the hills and up the mountain-side, and every afternoon, when he had echoed them back, the little dwarf grew more and more angry with the Dryad. Each day, from early morning till it was time for him to go back to his duties upon the rocky hillside, he searched the woods for her. He intended, if he met her, to pretend to be very sorry for what he had said, and he thought he might be able to play a trick upon her which would revenge him well. One day, while thus wandering among the trees, he met Old Pipes. The Echo-dwarf did not generally care to see or speak to ordinary people, but now he was so anxious to find the object of his search that he stopped and asked Old Pipes if he had seen the Dryad. The piper had not noticed the little fellow, and he looked down on him with some surprise.

"No," he said. "I have not seen her, and I have been looking everywhere for her."

"You!" cried the dwarf. "What do you wish with her?"

Old Pipes then sat down on a stone, so that he should be nearer the ear of his small companion, and he told what the Dryad had done for him.

When the Echo-dwarf heard that this was the man whose pipes he was obliged to echo back every day, he would have slain him on the spot had he been able. But as he was not able, he merely ground his teeth and listened to the rest of the story.

"I am looking for the Dryad now," Old Pipes continued, "on account of my aged mother. When I was old myself I did not notice how very aged my mother was; but now it shocks me to see how feeble and decrepit her years have caused her to become, and I am looking for the Dryad to ask her to make my mother younger, as she made me."

The eyes of the Echo-dwarf glistened. Here was a man who might help him in his plans.

"Your idea is a good one," he said to Old Pipes, "and it does you honor. But you should know that a Dryad can make no person younger but one who lets her out of her tree. However, you can manage the affair very easily. All you need do is to find the Dryad, tell her what you want, and request her to step into her tree and be shut up for a short time. Then you will go and bring your mother to the tree, she will open it, and everything will be as you wish. Is not this a good plan?"

"Excellent!" cried Old Pipes. "I will go instantly and search more diligently for the Dryad."

"Take me with you," said the Echo-dwarf. "You

can easily carry me on your strong shoulders, and I shall be glad to help you in any way that I can."

"Now, then," said the little fellow to himself, as Old Pipes carried him rapidly along, "if he persuades the Dryad to get into a tree,—and she is quite foolish enough to do it,—and then goes away to bring his mother, I shall take a stone or a club, and I will break off the key of that tree, so that nobody can ever turn it again. Then Mistress Dryad will see what she has brought upon herself by her behavior to me."

Before long they came to the great oak-tree in which the Dryad had lived, and, at a distance, they saw that beautiful creature herself coming toward them.

"How excellently well everything happens!" said the dwarf. "Put me down, and I will go. Your business with the Dryad is more important than mine, and you need not say anything about my having suggested your plan to you. I am willing that you should have all the credit of yourself."

Old Pipes put the Echo-dwarf upon the ground, but the little rogue did not go away. He concealed himself between some low, mossy rocks, and he was so much of their color that you would not have noticed him if you had been looking straight at him.

When the Dryad came up, Old Pipes lost no time in telling her about his mother, and what he wished her to do. At first the Dryad answered nothing, but stood looking very sadly at Old Pipes.

"Do you really wish me to go into my tree again?" she said. "I should dreadfully dislike to do it, for I don't know what might happen. It is not at all necessary, for I could make your mother younger at any time if she would give me the opportunity. I had already thought of making you still happier in this way, and several times I have waited about your cottage, hoping to meet your aged mother; but she never comes outside, and you know a Dryad cannot enter a house. I cannot imagine what put this idea into your head. Did you think of it yourself?"

"No, I cannot say that I did," answered Old Pipes. "A little dwarf whom I met in the woods proposed it to me."

"Oh!" cried the Dryad, "now I see through it all. It is the scheme of that vile Echo-dwarf—your enemy and mine. Where is he? I should like to see him."

"I think he has gone away," said Old Pipes.

"No, he has not," said the Dryad, whose quick eyes perceived the Echo-dwarf among the rocks. "There he is. Seize him and drag him out, I beg of you."

Old Pipes perceived the dwarf as soon as he was pointed out to him, and running to the rocks, he caught the little fellow by the leg and pulled him out.

"Now, then," cried the Dryad, who had opened the door of the great oak, "just stick him in there, and we will shut him up. Then I shall be safe from his mischief for the rest of the time I am free."

Old Pipes thrust the Echo-dwarf into the tree. The Dryad pushed the door shut. There was a clicking sound of bark and wood, and no one would have noticed that the big oak had ever had an opening in it.

"There," said the Dryad. "Now we need not be afraid of him. And I assure you, my good piper, that I shall be very glad to make your mother younger as soon as I can. Will you not ask her to come out and meet me?"

"Of course I will," cried Old Pipes. "I will do it without delay."

Then, the Dryad by his side, he hurried to his cottage. But when he mentioned the matter to his mother, the old woman became very angry indeed. She did not believe in Dryads; and if they really did exist, she knew they must be witches and sorceresses, and she would have nothing to do with them. If her son had ever allowed himself to be kissed by one of them he ought to be ashamed of himself. As to its doing him the least bit of good, she did not believe a word of it. He felt better than he used to feel, but that was very common. She had sometimes felt that way herself, and she forbade him ever to mention a Dryad to her again.

That afternoon Old Pipes, feeling very sad that his plan in regard to his mother had failed, sat down upon the rock and played upon his pipes. The pleasant sounds went down the valley and up the hills and mountain, but to the great surprise of some persons who happened to notice the fact, the notes were not echoed back from the rocky hillside, but from the woods on the side of the valley where Old Pipes lived.

The next day many of the villagers stopped in their work to listen to the echo of the pipes coming from the woods. The sound was not as clear and strong as it used to be when it was sent back from the rocky hillside, but it certainly came from among the trees. Such a thing as an echo changing its place in this way had never been heard of before, and nobody was able to explain how it could have happened. Old Pipes, however, knew very well that the sound came from the Echo-dwarf shut up in the great oak-tree. The sides of the tree were thin, the sound of the pipes could be heard through them, and the dwarf was obliged by the laws of his being to echo back those notes whenever they came to him. But Old Pipes thought he might get the Dryad in trouble if he let any one know that the Echo-dwarf was shut up in the tree, and so he wisely said nothing about it.

One day the two boys and the girl who had helped Old Pipes up the hill were playing in the woods. Stopping near the great oak-tree, they heard a sound of knocking within it, and then a voice plainly said:

"Let me out! let me out!"

For a moment the children stood still in astonishment, and then one of the boys exclaimed:

"Oh, it is a Dryad, like the one Old Pipes found! Let's let her out!"

"What are you thinking of?" cried the girl. "I am the oldest of all, and I am only thirteen. Do you wish to be turned into crawling babies? Run! run! run!"

And the two boys and the girl dashed down into the valley as fast as their legs could carry them. There was no desire in their youthful hearts to be made younger than they were. For fear that their parents might think it well that they should commence their careers anew, they never said a word about finding the Dryad tree.

As the summer days went on, Old Pipes's mother grew feebler and feebler. One day when her son was away, for he now frequently went into the woods to hunt or fish, or down into the valley to work, she arose from her knitting to prepare the simple dinner. But she felt so weak and tired that she was not able to do the work to which she had been so long accustomed. "Alas! alas!" she said, "the time has come when I am too old to work. My son will have to hire some one to come here and cook his meals, make his bed, and mend his clothes. Alas! alas! I had hoped that as long as I lived I should be able to do these things. But it is not so. I have grown utterly worthless, and some one else must prepare the dinner for my son. I wonder where he is." And tottering to the door, she went outside to look for him. She did not feel able to stand, and reaching the rustic chair, she sank into it, quite exhausted, and soon fell asleep.

The Dryad, who had often come to the cottage to see if she could find an opportunity of carrying out Old Pipes's affectionate design, now happened by, and seeing that the much-desired occasion had come, she stepped up quietly behind the old woman and gently kissed her on each cheek, and then as quietly disappeared.

In a few minutes the mother of Old Pipes awoke, and looking up at the sun, she exclaimed: "Why, it is almost dinner-time! My son will be here presently, and I am not ready for him." And rising to her feet, she hurried into the house, made the fire, set the meat and vegetables to cook, laid the cloth, and by the time her son arrived the meal was on the table.

"How a little sleep does refresh one!" she said to herself, as she was bustling about. She was a woman of very vigorous constitution, and at seventy had been a great deal stronger and more active than her son was at that age. The moment Old Pipes saw his mother, he knew that the Dryad had been there. But, while he felt happy as a king, he was too wise to say anything about her.

"It is astonishing how well I feel to-day!" said his mother, "and either my hearing has improved or you speak much more plainly than you have done of late."

The summer days went on and passed away, the leaves were falling from the trees, and the air was becoming cold.

"Nature has ceased to be lovely," said the Dryad, "and the night winds chill me. It is time for me to go back into my comfortable quarters in the great oak. But first I must pay another visit to the cottage of Old Pipes."

She found the piper and his mother sitting side by side on the rock in front of the door. The cattle were not to go to the mountain any more that season, and he was piping them down for the last time. Loud and merrily sounded the pipes of Old Pipes, and down the mountainside came the cattle, the cows by the easiest paths, the sheep by those not quite so easy, and the goats by the most difficult ones among the rocks, while from the great oak-tree were heard the echoes of the cheerful music.

"How happy they look, sitting there together!" said the Dryad, "and I don't believe it will do them a bit of harm to be still younger." And moving quietly up behind them, she first kissed Old Pipes on his cheek, and then his mother.

Old Pipes, who had stopped playing, knew what it was, but he did not move, and said nothing. His mother, thinking that her son had kissed her, turned to him with a smile and kissed him in return. Then she arose and went into the cottage, a vigorous woman of sixty, followed by her son, erect and happy, and twenty years younger than herself.

The Dryad sped away to the woods, shrugging her shoulders as she felt the cool evening wind.

When she reached the great oak, she turned the key and opened the door. "Come out," she said to the Echo-dwarf, who sat blinking within. "Winter is coming on, and I want the comfortable shelter of my tree for myself. The cattle have come down from the mountain for the last time this year, the pipes will no longer sound, and you can go to your rocks and have a holiday until next spring."

Upon hearing these words the dwarf skipped quickly out, and the Dryad entered the tree and pulled the door shut after her. "Now, then," she said to herself, "he can break off the key if he likes. It does not matter to me. Another will grow out next spring. And although the good piper made me no promise, I know that when the warm days arrive next year, he will come and let me out again."

The Echo-dwarf did not stop to break the key of the tree. He was too happy at being released to think of anything else, and he hastened as fast as he could to his home on the rocky hillside.

The Dryad was not mistaken when she trusted in the piper. When the warm days came again he went to the oak-tree to let her out. But, to his sorrow and surprise, he found the great tree lying upon the ground. A winter storm had blown it down, and it lay with its trunk shattered and split. And what became of the Dryad, no one ever knew.

The Castle of Bim

LORIS WAS a little girl, about eleven years old, who lived with her father, in a very small house among the mountains of a distant land. He was sometimes a woodcutter, and sometimes a miner, or a ploughman, or a stone-breaker. Being an industrious man he would work at anything he could do when a chance offered, but as there was not much work to do in that part of the country, poor Jorn often found it very hard to make a living for himself and Loris.

One day, when he had gone out early to look for work, Loris was in her little sleeping-room under the roof, braiding her hair. Although she was so poor, Loris always tried to make herself look as neat as she could, for that pleased her father. She was just tying the ribbon on the end of the long braid, when she heard a knock at the door below. "In one second," she said to herself, "I will go. I must tie this ribbon tightly, for it would never do to lose it."

And so she tied it, and ran down-stairs to the door; there was no one there.

"Oh, it is too bad!" cried Loris. "Perhaps it was some one with a job for father. He told me always to be very careful about answering a knock at the door, for there was no knowing when some one might come with a good job, and now some one has come, and gone," cried Loris, looking about in every direction for the person who had knocked. "Oh, there he is! How could he have got away so far in such a short time? I must run after him."

So away she ran as fast as she could, after a man she saw, walking away from the cottage in the direction of a forest.

"Oh, dear!" she said, as she ran, "How fast he walks! and he is such a short man, too! He is going right to the hut of Laub, that wicked Laub, who is always trying to get away work from father, and he came first to our house, but thought there was nobody at home."

Loris ran and ran, but the short man did walk very fast. However, she gradually gained on him, and just as he reached Laub's door, she seized him by the coat. "Stop—sir, please," she said, scarcely able to speak, she was so out of breath. The man turned and looked at her. He was a very short man, indeed, for he scarcely reached to Loris' waist.

"What do you want?" he said, looking up at her.

"Oh, sir!" she gasped, "you came to our house first,—and I came to the door—almost as quick as I could—and if it's any work—father wants work—ever so bad."

"Yes," said the short man, "but Laub wants work too. He is very poor."

"Yes, sir," said Loris, "but—but you came for father first."

"True," said the short man, "but nobody answered my knock, and now I am here. Laub has four young children, and sometimes they have nothing to eat. It is never so bad with you, is it?"

"No, sir," said Loris.

"Your father has work sometimes, is it not so?"

"Yes, sir," answered Loris.

"Laub is often without work for weeks, and he has four children. Shall I go back with you, or knock here?"

"Knock," said Loris softly.

The short man knocked at the door, and instantly, there was heard a great scuffling and hubbub within. Shortly all was quiet, and then a voice said, "Come in."

"He did not wait so long for me," thought Loris.

The short man opened the door, and went in, Loris following him. In a bed, in the corner of the room, were four children; their heads just appearing above a torn sheet which was pulled up to their chins.

"Hello! what's the matter?" said the short man, advancing to the bed.

"Please, sir," said the oldest child, a girl of about the age of Loris, with tangled hair and sharp black eyes, "we are all sick, and very poor, and our father has no work. If you can give us a little money to buy bread—"

"All sick, eh!" said the short man. "Any particular disease?"

"We don't know about diseases, sir," said the girl, "we've never been to school."

"No doubt of that," said the man. "I have no money to give you, but you can tell your father that if he will come to the mouth of the Ragged Mine, to-morrow morning, he can have a job of work which will pay him well." So saying he went out. Loris followed him, but he simply waved his hand to her, and in a few minutes was lost in the forest.

Loris looked sadly after him, and then walked slowly towards her home.

The moment their visitors had gone, the Laub children sprang out of bed, as lively as crickets.

"Ha! Ha!" cried the oldest girl. "She came after him to get it, and he wouldn't give it to her, and father's got it. Served her right, the horrid thing!" and all the children shouted, "Horrid thing!" One of the boys now ran out, and threw a stone after Loris, and then they sat down to finish eating a meat pie, which had been given them.

"Well," said Jorn, that evening when Loris told him what had happened. "I'm sorry, for I found but little work to-day, but it can't be helped. You did all you could."

"No, father," said Loris. "I might have gone to the door quicker."

"That may be," said Jorn, "and I hope you will never keep any one waiting again."

Two or three days after this, as Loris was stooping over the fire, in the back room of the cottage, preparing her dinner, she heard a knock.

Springing to her feet, she dropped the pan she held in her hand, and made a dash at the front door, pulling it open with a tremendous fling. No one should go away this time.

"Hello! Ho! ho!" cried a person outside, giving a skip backwards. "Do you open doors by lightning here?"

"No, sir," said Loris; "but I didn't want to keep you waiting."

"I should think not," said the other; "why I had hardly begun to knock."

This visitor was a middle-sized man, very slight, and, at first sight, of a youthful appearance. But his hair was either powdered or gray, and it was difficult to know whether he was old or young. His face was long and smooth, and he nearly always looked as if he was just going to burst out laughing. He was dressed in a silken suit of light green, pink, pale yellow and sky blue, but all the colors were very much faded. On his head was stuck a tall orange-colored hat, with a lemon-colored feather.

"Is your father in?" said this strange personage.

"No, sir," said Loris. "He will be here this evening, and I can give him any message you may leave for him."

"I haven't any message," said the other. "I want to see him."

"You can see him about sun-set," said Loris, "if you will come then."

"I don't want to come again. I think I'll wait," said the man.

Loris said, "Very well," but she wondered what he would do all the afternoon. She brought out a stool for him to sit upon, for it was not very pleasant in the house, and there he sat for some time looking at the chicken-house, where there were no chickens; and the cow-house, where there was no cow; and the pig-sty, where there were no pigs. Then he skipped up to the top of a little hillock near by, and surveyed the landscape. Loris kept her eye upon him, to see that he did not go away without leaving a message, and went on with her cooking.

When her dinner was ready she thought it only right to ask him to have some. She did not want to do it, but she could not see how she could help it.

She had been taught good manners. So she went to the door, and called him, and he instantly came skipping to her.

"I thought you might like to have some dinner, sir," she said. "I haven't much, but——"

"Two people don't want much," he said, "where shall we have it? In the house, or will you spread the cloth out here on the grass?"

"There's not much use of spreading a cloth, sir," she said, "I have only one potato, and some salt."

"That's not a dinner," said the other cheerfully, "a dinner is soup, meat, some vegetables (besides potatoes, and there ought to be two of them, at least), some bread, some cheese, pudding and fruit."

"But, I haven't got all that, sir," said Loris, with her eyes wide open at this astonishing description of a dinner.

"Well then, if you haven't got them the next best thing is to go and get them."

Loris smiled faintly. "I couldn't do that, sir," she said, "I have no money."

"Well then, if you can't go the next best thing is for me to go. The village is not far away—just wait dinner a little while for me," and so saying he skipped away at a great pace.

Loris did not wait for him, but ate her potato and salt. "I'm glad he is able to buy his own dinner," she said, "but I'm afraid he won't come back. I wish he had left a message." But she need not have feared.

In a half-hour the queer man came back, bearing a great basket covered with a cloth. The latter he spread on the ground, and then set out all the things he had said were necessary to make up a dinner. He prepared a place at one end of the cloth for Loris, and one at the other end for himself.

"Sit down," said he, seating himself on the grass, "Don't let things get cold."

"I've had my dinner," said Loris. "This is yours."

"Whenever you're ready to begin," said the man, lying back on the grass and looking placidly up to the sky, "I'll begin. But not until then."

Loris saw he was in earnest, and, as she was a sensible girl, she sat down at the end of the cloth.

"That's right," gaily cried the queer man, sitting up again, "I was a little afraid you'd be obstinate and then I should have starved."

When the meal was over, Loris said, "I never had such a good dinner in my life."

The man looked at her and laughed. "This is a funny world, isn't it?" said he.

"Awfully funny!" replied Loris, laughing.

"You don't know what I am, do you?" said the man to Loris, as she gathered up the dishes and put them, with what was left of the meal, into the basket.

"No, sir; I do not," answered Loris.

"I am a Ninkum," said the other. "Did you ever meet with one before?"

"No, sir, never," said Loris.

"I am very glad to hear that," he said. "It's so pleasant to be fresh and novel." And then he went walking around the house again, looking at everything he had seen before. Soon he laid himself down on the grass, near the house, with one leg thrown over the other and his hands clasped under his head. For a long time he lay in this way, looking up at the sky and the clouds. Then he turned his head, and said to Loris, who was sewing by the door-step:

"Did you ever think how queer it would be if everything in the world were reversed; if the ground were soft and blue, like the sky, and if the sky were covered with dirt and chips and grass, and if fowls and animals walked about on it, like flies sticking to a ceiling?"

"I never thought of such a thing in my life," said Loris.

"I often do," said the Ninkum, "It expands the mind."

For the whole afternoon the Ninkum lay on his back, and expanded his mind, and then, about sunset Loris saw her father returning. She ran to meet him, and told him of the Ninkum who was waiting to see him. Jorn hurried to the house, for he felt sure that his visitor must have an important job of work for him, as he had waited so long.

"I am glad you have come," said the Ninkum, "I wanted to see you very much, for two things. The first was that we might have supper. I'm dreadfully hungry, and I know there's enough in that basket for us all. The second thing can wait; it's business."

So Loris and the Ninkum spread out the remains of the dinner, and the three made a hearty supper. Jorn was highly pleased; he had expected to come home to a very different meal from this.

"Now, then," said the Ninkum, "We'll talk about the business."

"You have some work for me, I suppose," said Jorn.

"No," said the Ninkum, "none that I know of. What I want is for you to go into partnership with me."

"Partnership!" cried Jorn, "I don't understand you. What kind of work could we do together?"

"None at all," said the Ninkum, "for I never work. Your part of the partnership will be to chop wood, and mine, and plough, and do just what you do now. I will live here with you, and will provide the food, and the clothes, and the fuel, and the pocket-money for the three of us."

"But you couldn't live here," cried Loris, "our house is so poor, and there is no room for you."

"There need be no trouble about that," said the Ninkum, "I can build a room, right here, on this side of the house. I never work," he said to Jorn, "but I hate idleness. So what I want is to go into partnership with a person who will work,—an industrious person like you. Then my conscience will be at ease. Please agree as quickly as you can, for it's beginning to grow dark, and I hate to walk in the dark."

Jorn did not hesitate. He agreed instantly to go into partnership with the Ninkum, and the latter, after bidding them good-night, skipped gaily away.

The next day, he returned with carpenters, and laborers, and lumber, and timber, and furniture, and bedding, and a large and handsome room was built for him, on one side of the house, and he came to live with Jorn and Loris. For several days he had workmen putting a fence around the yard, and building a new cow-house, a new chicken-house, and a new pig-sty. He bought a cow, pigs and chickens, had flowers planted in front of the house, and made everything look very neat and pretty.

"Now," said he one day to Loris and Jorn as they were eating supper together, "I'll tell you something, I was told to keep it a secret, but I hate secrets; I think they all ought to be told as soon as possible. Ever so much trouble has been made by secrets. The one I have is this: That dwarf, who came here, and then went and hired old Laub to work in his mine—"

"Was that a dwarf?" asked Loris, much excited.

"Yes, indeed," said the Ninkum, "a regular one.

Didn't you notice how short he was? Well, he told me all about his coming here. The dwarfs in the Ragged Mine found a deep hole, with lots of gold at the bottom of it, but it steamed and smoked and was too hot for dwarfs. So the king dwarf sent out the one you saw, and told him to hire the first miner he could find, to work in the deep hole, but not to tell him how hot it was until he had made his contract. So the dwarf had to come first for you, Jorn, for you lived nearest the mine, but he hoped he would not find you, for he knew you were a good man. That was the reason he just gave one knock, and hurried on to Laub's house. And then he told me how Loris ran after him, and how good she was to agree to let him give the work to Laub, when she thought he needed it more than her father. 'Now,' says he to me, 'I want to do something for that family, and I don't know anything better that could happen to a man like Jorn, than to go into partnership with a Ninkum.''

At these words, Jorn looked over the well-spread supper-table, and he thought the dwarf was certainly right.

"So that's the way I came to live here," said the Ninkum, "and I like it first-rate."

"I wish I could go and see the dwarfs working in their mines," said Loris.

"I'll take you," exclaimed the Ninkum. "It's not a long walk from here. We can go to-morrow."

Jorn gave his consent, and the next morning Loris and the Ninkum set out for the Ragged Mine. The entrance was a great jagged hole in the side of a mountain, and the inside of the mine had also a very rough and torn appearance. It belonged to a colony of dwarfs, and ordinary mortals seldom visited it, but the Ninkum had no difficulty in obtaining admission. Making their way slowly along the rough and sombre tunnel, Loris and he saw numbers of dwarfs, working with pick and shovel, in search of precious minerals.

Soon they met the dwarf who had come to Jorn's house, and he seemed glad to see Loris again. He led her about to various parts of the mine, and showed her the heaps of gold and silver and precious stones, which had been dug out of the rocks around them.

The Ninkum had seen these things before, and so he thought he would go and look for the hot hole, where Laub was working; that would be a novelty.

He soon found the hole, and just as he reached it, Laub appeared at its opening, slowly climbing up a ladder.

He looked very warm and tired, and throwing some gold ore upon the ground, from a basket which he carried on his back, he sat down and wiped the perspiration from his forehead.

"That is warm work, Laub," said the Ninkum, pleasantly.

"Warm!" said Laub, gruffly, "hot—hot as fire. Why the gold down at the bottom of that hole burns your fingers when you pick it up. If I hadn't made a contract with these rascally dwarfs to work here for forty-one days, I wouldn't stay here another minute, but you can't break a contract you make with dwarfs."

"It's a pretty hard thing to have to work here, that is true," said the Ninkum, "but you owe your ill-fortune to yourself. It's all because you're known to be so ill-natured and wicked. When the dwarf was sent to hire a man to come and work in this hole, he had to go to Jorn's house first because that was the nearest place, but he just gave one knock there, and hurried away, hoping he didn't hear, for it would be a pity to have a good man like Jorn working in a place like this. Then he went after you, for he knew you deserved to be punished by this kind of work."

As the Ninkum said this, Laub's face grew black with rage.

"So that's the truth!" he cried, "when I get out of this place, I'll crush every bone in the body of that sneaking Jorn," and, so saying he rushed down into the hot hole.

"Perhaps I ought not to have told him all that," said the Ninkum, as he walked away, "but I hate secrets, they always make mischief."

When he joined Loris, the little girl said, "Let us go out of this place now. I have seen nearly every thing, and it is so dark and gloomy."

Taking leave of the kind dwarf, the two made their way out of the mine.

"I do not like such gloomy places any better than you do," said the Ninkum. "Disagreeable things are always happening in them. I like to have things bright and lively. I'll tell you what would be splendid! To make a visit to the Castle of Bim."

"What is that, and where is it?" asked Loris.

"It's the most delightful place in the whole world," said the Ninkum. "While you're there you do nothing and see nothing but what is positively charming, and every body is just as happy and gay as can be. It's all life and laughter, and perfect delight. I know you would be overjoyed if you were there."

"I should like very much to go," said Loris, "if father would let me."

"I'll go and ask him this minute," said the Ninkum. "I know where he is working. You can run home, and I will go to him, and then come and tell you what he says."

So Loris ran home, and the Ninkum went to the place where Jorn was cutting wood. "Jorn," said the Ninkum, "suppose that every thing in the world were reversed; that you chopped wood, standing on your head, and that you split your axe, instead of the log you struck. Would not that be peculiar?"

"Such things could not be," said Jorn, "what is the good of talking about them?"

"I think a great deal about such matters," said the Ninkum. "They expand my mind, and now, Jorn, reversibly speaking will you let Loris go with me to the Castle of Bim?"

"Where is that?" asked Jorn.

"It is not far from here. I think we could go in half a day. I would get a horse in the village."

"And how long would you stay?"

"Well, I don't know. A week or two, perhaps. Come, now, Jorn, reversibly speaking, may she go?"

"No, indeed," said Jorn, "on no account shall she go. I could not spare her."

"All right," said the Ninkum, "I will not keep you from your work any longer. Good-morning."

As soon as he was out of Jorn's sight, the Ninkum began to run home as fast as he could.

"Get ready, Loris," he cried, when he reached the house. "Your father says, reversibly speaking, that on every account you must go. He can well spare you."

"But must we go now?" said Loris. "Cannot we wait until he comes home, and go to-morrow?"

"No, indeed," said the Ninkum. "There will be obstacles to our starting to-morrow. So let us hasten to the village, and hire a horse. Your father will get along nicely here by himself, and he will be greatly pleased with your improvement when you return from the Castle of Bim."

So Loris, who was really much pleased with the idea of the journey, hastened to get ready, and having put the house-key under the front door-stone, she and the Ninkum went to the village, where they got a horse and started for the Castle of Bim.

The Ninkum rode in front, Loris sat on a pillow behind, and the horse trotted along gaily. The Ninkum was in high good spirits, and passed the time in telling Loris of all the delightful things she would see in the Castle of Bim.

Late in the afternoon, they came in sight of a vast castle, which rose up at the side of the road like a little mountain.

"Hurrah!" cried the Ninkum, as he spurred the horse. "I knew we were nearly there!"

Loris was very glad that they had reached the castle, for she was getting tired of riding, and when the Ninkum drew up in front of the great portals, she felt sure that she was going to see wonderful things, for the door, to begin with, was, she felt sure, the biggest door in the whole world.

"You need not get off," said the porter, who stood by the door, to the Ninkum, who was preparing to dismount, "you can ride right in."

Accordingly, the Ninkum and Loris rode right in to the castle through the front door. Inside, they found themselves in a high and wide hall-way paved with stone, which led back to what appeared to be an inner court. Riding to the end of this hall, they stopped in the doorway there, and looked out. In the centre of the court, which was very large, there stood side by side, and about twenty feet apart, two great upright posts, like the trunks of tall pine trees. Across these, near their tops, rested a thick and heavy horizontal pole, and on this pole a giant was practising gymnastics.

Hanging by his hands, he would draw himself up, until his chin touched the pole. And again and again he did this, until the Ninkum said in a whisper, "Twelve times. I did not think he could do it."

The giant now drew up his legs, and threw them over the bar, above his head. Then, by a vigorous effort, he turned himself entirely over the bar, and hung beneath it by his hands. After stopping a minute or two to breathe, he drew up his legs again, and putting them under the bar, between his hands as boys do when they "skin the cat," he turned partly over, and hung in this position.

His face was now turned toward the doorway, and he first noticed his visitors.

"Hello!" said he to the Ninkum. "Could you do that?"

"Not on that pole," answered the Ninkum, smiling.

"I should think not," said the giant, dropping to his feet, and puffing a little. "Ten years ago, when I did not weigh so much, I could draw myself up twenty-seven times. Come in with me and have some supper. Is that your little daughter?"

"No," said the Ninkum, "I am her guardian for the present."

"Ride right up-stairs," said the giant. "My wife is up there and she will take care of the little girl."

"I am afraid," said the Ninkum, "that my horse cannot jump up those great steps."

"Of course not," said the giant. "Let me help you up, and then I will go down and bring your horses."

"Oh, that won't be necessary," said the Ninkum, and Loris laughed at the idea.

"You may want to look at the house," said the giant, "and then you will need them."

So the giant took the Ninkum and Loris up-stairs, and then came down, and brought up the horses. The upper story was as vast and spacious as the lower part of the castle, and by a window the giant's wife sat, darning a stocking.

As they approached her, the Ninkum whispered to Loris: "If there were such holes in my stockings I should fall through." The giantess was very glad to see Loris, and she took her up in her hand, and kissed her, very much as a little girl would kiss a canary bird. Then the giant children were sent for—two big boys and a baby girl, who thought Loris was so lovely that she would have squeezed her to death, if her mother had allowed her to take the little visitor in her hands.

During supper, Loris and the Ninkum sat in chairs with long legs, like stilts, which the giant had had made for his men and women visitors. They had to be very careful, lest they should tip over and break their necks.

After supper, they sat in the great upper hall, and the giant got out his guitar and sang them a song.

"I hope there are not many more verses," whispered the Ninkum to Loris, "My bones are almost shaken apart."

"How did you like that?" asked the giant, when he had finished.

"It was very nice," said the Ninkum, "it reminded me of something I once heard before; I think it was a wagon-load of copper pots, rolling down a mountain, but I am not sure."

The giant thanked him, and soon after, they all went to bed. Loris slept in the room with the giantess, on a high shelf where the children could not reach her.

Just before they went to their rooms the Ninkum said to Loris:

"Do you know that I don't believe this is the Castle of Bim?"

"It didn't seem to be like the place you told me about," said Loris, "but what are we to do?"

"Nothing, but to go to bed," said the Ninkum. "They are very glad to see us, and to-morrow we will bid them good-bye, and push on to the Castle of Bim."

With this, the Ninkum jumped on his horse, and rode to his room.

The next day, after they had gone over the castle and seen all its sights, the Ninkum told the giant that he and Loris must pursue their journey to the Castle of Bim.

"What is that?" said the giant, and when the Ninkum proceeded to describe it to him, he became very much interested.

"Ho! Ho! good wife!" he cried, "suppose we go with these friends to the Castle of Bim. It must be a very pleasant place, and the exercise will do me good. I'm dreadfully tired of gymnastics. What do you say? We can take the children."

The giantess thought it would be a capital idea, and so they all put on their hats and caps, and started off, leaving the castle in charge of the giants' servants, who were people of common size.

They journeyed all that day. Loris and the Ninkum riding ahead, followed by the giant, then, by the giantess carrying the baby, and lastly the two giant boys with a basket of provisions between them.

That night they slept on the ground, under some trees, and the Ninkum admitted that the Castle of Bim was a good deal further off than he had supposed it to be.

Toward afternoon of the next day they found

themselves on some high land, and coming to the edge of a bluff, they saw in the plain below, a beautiful city. The giant was struck with admiration.

"I have seen many a city," said he, "but I never saw one so sensibly and handsomely laid out as that. The people who built that place knew just what they wanted."

"Do you see that great building in the centre of the city?" cried the Ninkum. "Well, that is the Castle of Bim. Let us hurry down." So, away they all started, at their best speed, for the city.

They had scarcely reached one of the outer gates, when they were met by a citizen on horseback, followed by two or three others on foot. The horseman greeted them kindly, and said that he had been sent to meet them. "We shall be very glad," he said to the Ninkum, "to have you and the little girl come into our city tonight, but if those giants were to enter, the people, especially the children, would throng the streets to see them, and many would unavoidably be trampled to death. There is a great show tent out here, where they can very comfortably pass the night, and to-morrow we will have the streets cleared, and the people kept within doors. Then these great visitors will be made welcome to walk in and view the city."

The giants agreed to this, and they were conducted to the tent, where they were made very comfortable, while the Ninkum and Loris were taken into the city, and lodged in the house of the citizen who had come to meet them.

The next day the giants entered the city, and the windows and doors in the streets which they passed through, were crowded with spectators.

The giant liked the city better and better, as he walked through it. Everything was so admirably pleasing, and in such perfect order. The others enjoyed themselves very much, too, and Loris was old enough to understand the beauty and conveniences of the things she saw around her.

Towards the end of the day, the Ninkum came to her.

"Do you know," said he, "that the Castle of Bim is not here? That large building is used by the governors of the city. And what a queer place it is! Everything that they do turns out just right. I saw a man set a rat-trap and what do you think? He caught the rat! I could not help laughing. It is very funny."

"But what are you going to do?" asked Loris.

"We will stay here to-night," said the Ninkum, "they are very kind,—and to-morrow we will go on to the Castle of Bim."

The next day, therefore, our party again set out on their journey. The Ninkum had told the citizen, who had entertained him, where they were going and his accounts of the wonderful castle induced this worthy man to go with him.

"In our city," said he, "we try to be governed in everything by the ordinary rules of common sense. In this way we get along very comfortably and pleasantly, and everything seems to go well with us. But we are always willing to examine into the merits of things which are new to us, and so I would like to go to this curious castle, and come back and report what I have seen to my fellow-citizens."

His company was gladly accepted, and all set out in high good humor, the citizen riding by the side of Loris and the Ninkum.

But when they had gone several miles, the giantess declared that she believed she would go back home. The baby was getting very heavy, and the boys were tired. The giant could tell her about the Castle of Bim when he came home.

So the giantess turned back with her children, her husband kissing her good-bye, and assuring her that he would not let her go back by herself if he did not feel certain that no one would molest her on the way.

The rest of the party now went on at a good pace, the giant striding along as fast as the horses could trot. The Ninkum did not seem to know the way as well as he said he did. He continually desired to turn to the right, and, when the others inquired if he was sure that he ought to do this, he said that the best thing a person could do when a little in doubt was to turn to the right.

The citizen did not like this method of reasoning, and he was about to make an objection to it, when a man was perceived, sitting, in doleful plight, by the side of the road. The Ninkum who was very kind-hearted, rode up to him, to inquire what had happened to him, but the moment the man raised his head, and before he had time to say a word, Loris slipped off her horse and threw her arms around his neck.

"Oh father! father!" she cried. "How came you here?"

It was indeed, Jorn, ragged, wounded and exhausted.

In a moment everyone set to work to relieve him. Loris ran for water and bathed his face and hands; the citizen gave him some wine, from a flask; the giant produced some great pieces of bread and meat; and the Ninkum asked him questions.

Jorn soon felt refreshed and strengthened, and then he told his story. He had been greatly troubled, when he found that Loris had gone away against his express orders.

"Why father," cried Loris, at this point, "you said I could go."

"Never," said Jorn, "I said you could not go."

"Reversibly speaking," said the Ninkum smiling, "he consented, that was the way I put the question to him. If I had not put it in that way, I should have told a lie."

Everybody looked severely at the Ninkum, and Loris was very angry, but her father patted her on the head, and went on with his story. He would have followed the Ninkum and his daughter, but he did not know what road they had taken, and as they were on a horse he could not in any case, expect to catch up with them.

So he waited, hoping they would soon return, but, before long he was very glad that Loris was away.

The wicked Laub, who, in some manner, had found out that he had been made to work in the dwarf's mine instead of Jorn, who had been considered too good for such disagreeable labor, had become so enraged, that he broke his contract with the dwarfs, and, instead of continuing his work in the mine, had collected a few of his depraved companions, and had made an attack upon Jorn's house.

The doors had been forced, poor Jorn had been dragged forth, beaten, and forced to fly, while Laub and his companions took possession of the house, and everything in it.

"But how could you wander so far, dear father?" asked Loris.

"It is not far," said Jorn, "our home is not many miles away."

"Then you have been going in a circle," said the

citizen to the Ninkum, "and you are now very near the point you started from."

"That seems to be the case," said the Ninkum, smiling.

"But we won't talk about it now," said the citizen. "We must see what we can do for this poor man. He must have his house again."

"I would have asked the dwarfs to help me," said Jorn, "but I believe they would have killed Laub and the others if they had resisted, and I didn't want any blood shed."

"No," said the citizen. "I think we can manage it better than that. Our large friend here will be able to get these people out of your house without killing them."

"Oh, yes," said the giant, "I'll attend to that."

Jorn being now quite ready to travel, the party proceeded, and soon reached his house.

When Laub perceived the approach of Jorn and his friends, he barricaded all the doors and windows, and, with his companions prepared to resist all attempts to enter.

But his efforts were useless. The giant knelt down before the house, and having easily removed the door, he thrust in his arm, and sweeping it around the room, easily caught three of the invaders.

He then put his other arm through the window of the Ninkum's room, and soon pulled out Laub, taking no notice of his kicks and blows.

The giant then tied the four rascals in a bunch by the feet, and laid them on the grass.

"Now," said the citizen to the Ninkum, "as there seems to be nothing more to be done for this good man and his daughter, suppose you tell me the way to the Castle of Bim. I think I can find it, if I have good directions, and I do not wish to waste any more time."

"I do not know the exact way," answered the Ninkum.

"What!" cried the other, "have you never been there?"

"No," said the Ninkum.

"Well, then, did not the person who told you about it, tell you the way?"

"No one ever told me about it," replied the Ninkum. "I have thought a great deal on the subject, and I feel sure that there must be such a place, and the way to find it is to go and look for it."

"Well," said the citizen, smiling, "you are a true Ninkum. I suppose we have all thought of some place where everything shall be just as we want it to be, and I don't believe any of us will find that place. I am going home."

"And I too," said the giant, "and on my way I will stop at the Ragged Mine, and leave those fellows to the care of the dwarfs. They will see that they molest honest men no more."

"And I think I will go too," said the Ninkum, "I liked this place very much, but I am getting tired of it now."

"That will be a good thing for you to do," said the citizen, who had heard the story of how the Ninkum had been sent to Jorn and Loris, as a reward. "You have lived for a time with these good people, and have been of some service to them, but I am quite sure they now feel that partnership with a Ninkum is a very dangerous thing, and should not be kept up too long."

"No doubt that's true," said the Ninkum. "Good-bye, my friends. I will give you my room and everything that is in it."

"You have been very kind to us," said Loris.

"Yes," said Jorn, "and you got me work that will last a long time."

"I did what I could," cried the Ninkum, mounting his horse, and gaily waving his hat around his head, "and, reversibly speaking, I took you to the Castle of Bim."

The Magician's Daughter and the High-Born Boy

THERE WAS once a great castle which belonged to a magician. It stood upon a high hill, with a wide courtyard in front of it, and the fame of its owner spread over the whole land. He was a very wise and skillful magician, as well as a kind and honest man, and people of all degrees came to him, to help him out of their troubles.

But he gradually grew very old, and at last he died. His only descendant was a daughter, thirteen years of age, named Filamina, and everybody wondered what would happen, now that the great magician was dead.

But one day, Filamina came out on the broad front steps of the castle, and made a little speech to all the giants, and afrits, and fairies, and genii, and dwarfs, and gnomes, and elves, and pigmies, and other creatures of that kind, who had always been in the service of the old magician, to do his bidding when some wonderful thing was to be accomplished.

"Now that my poor father is dead," said she, "I think it is my duty to carry on the business. So you will all do what I tell you to do, just as you used to obey my father. If any persons come who want anything done, I will attend to them."

The giants and fairies, and all the others, were very glad to hear Filamina say this, for they all liked her, and they were tired of being idle.

Then an afrit arose from the sunny stone on which he had been lying, and said that there were six people outside of the gate, who had come to see if there was a successor to the magician, who could help them out of their trouble.

"You can bring them into the Dim-lit Vault," said Filamina, "but, first, I will go in and get ready for them."

The Dim-lit Vault was a vast apartment, with a vaulted ceiling, where the old magician used to see the people who came to him. All around the walls or shelves, and on stands and tables, in various parts of the room, were the strange and wonderful instruments of magic that he used.

There was a great table in the room, covered with parchments and old volumes of magic lore. At one end of the table was the magician's chair, and in this Filamina seated herself, first piling several cushions on the seat, to make herself high enough.

"Now, then," said she, to the afrit in attendance, "everything seems ready, but you must light something to make a mystic smell. That iron lamp at the other end of the room will do. Do you know what to pour into it?"

The afrit did not know, but he thought he could find something, so he examined the bottles on the shelves, and taking down one of them, he poured some of its contents into the lamp and lighted it. In an instant there was an explosion, and a piece of the heavy lamp just grazed the afrit's head.

"Don't try that again," said Filamina. "You will be hurt. Let a ghost come in. He can't be injured."

So a ghost came in, and he got another iron lamp, and tried the stuff from another bottle. This blew up, the same as the other, and several pieces of the lamp went right through the ghost's body, but of course it made no difference to him. He tried again, and this time he found something which smelt extremely mystical.

"Now call them in," said Filamina, and the six persons who were in trouble entered the room. Filamina took a piece of paper and a pencil, and asked them, in turn, what they wished her to do for them. The first was a merchant, in great grief because he had lost a lot of rubies, and he wanted to know where to find them.

"How many of them were there?" asked Filamina of the unlucky merchant.

"Two quarts," said the merchant. "I measured them a few days ago. Each one of them was as large as a cherry."

"A big cherry?" asked Filamina.

"Yes," said the merchant. "The biggest kind of a cherry."

"Well," said Filamina, putting all this down on her paper, "you can come again in a week, and I will see what I can do for you."

The next was a beautiful damsel who had lost her lover.

"What kind of a person is he?" asked Filamina.

"Oh," said the beautiful damsel, "he is handsomer than tongue can tell. Tall, magnificent, and splendid in every way. He is more graceful than a deer, and stronger than a lion. His hair is like flowing silk, and his eyes like the noon-day sky."

"Well, don't cry any more," said Filamina. "I think we shall soon find him. There can't be many of that kind. Come again in a week, if you please."

The next person was a covetous king, who was very anxious to possess the kingdom next to his own.

"The only difficulty is this," he said, his greedy eyes twinkling as he spoke, "there is an old king on the throne, and there is a very young heir—a mere baby. If they were both dead, I would be the next of kin, and would have the kingdom. I don't want to have them killed instantly. I want something that will make them sicker, and sicker, and sicker, till they die."

"Then you would like something suitable for a very old man, and something for a very young child?" said Filamina.

"That is exactly it," replied the covetous king.

"Very well," said Filamina; "come again in a week, and I will see what I can do for you."

The covetous king did not want to wait so long, but there was no help for it, and he went away.

Next came forward a young man, who wanted to find out how to make gold out of old iron bars and horseshoes. He had tried many different plans, but could not succeed. After him came a general, who could never defeat the great armies which belonged to the neighboring nations. He wished to get something which would insure victory to his army. Each of these was told to come again in a week, when his case would be attended to.

The last person was an old woman, who wanted to know a good way to make root-beer. She had sold root-beer for a long time, but it was not very good, and it made people feel badly, so that her custom was falling off. It was really necessary, she said, for her to have a good business, in order that she might support her sons and daughters, and send her grandchildren to school.

"Poor woman!" said Filamina. "I will do my best for you. Do you live far away?"

"Oh, yes," said the old woman, "a weary way."

"Well, then, I will have you taken home, and I will send for you in a week."

Thereupon, calling two tall giants, she told them to carry the old woman home in a sedan-chair, which they bore between them.

When the visitors had all gone, Filamina called in her servants and read to them the list she had made.

"As for this merchant," she said, "some of you gnomes ought to find his rubies. You are used to precious stones. Take a big cherry with you, and try to find two quarts of rubies of that size. A dozen fairies can go and look for the handsome lover of the beautiful damsel. You'll be sure to know him if you see him. A genie can examine the general's army and see what's the matter with it. Four or five dwarfs, used to working with metals, can take some horseshoes and try to make gold ones of them. Do any of you know a good disease for an old person, and a good disease for a baby?"

An elf suggested rheumatism for the old person, and Filamina herself thought of colic for the baby.

"Go and mix me," she said to an afrit, "some

rheumatism and some colic in a bottle. I am going to make that greedy king take it himself. As for the root-beer," she continued, "those of you who think you can do it, can take any of the stuff you find on the shelves here, and try to make good root-beer out of it. To-morrow, we will see if any of you have made beer that is really good. I will give a handsome reward to the one who first finds out how it ought to be made."

Thereupon, Filamina went up to her own room to take a nap, while quite a number of fairies, giants, dwarfs and others set to work to try and make good root-beer. They made experiments with nearly all the decoctions and chemicals they found on the shelves, or stored away in corners, and they boiled, and soaked, and mixed, and stirred, until far into the night.

It was a moonlight night, and one of the gnomes went from the Dim-lit Vault, where his companions were working away, into the court-yard, and there he met the ghost, who was gliding around by himself.

"I'll tell you what it is," said the gnome, "I don't want to be here to-morrow morning, when that stuff is to be tasted. They're making a lot of dreadful messes in there. I'm going to run away, till it's all over."

"It doesn't make any difference to me," said the ghost, "for I wouldn't be asked to drink anything; but, if you're going to run away, I don't mind going with you. I haven't got anything to do." So off the two started together, out of the great gate.

"Hold up!" soon cried the gnome, who was running as fast as his little legs would carry him. "Can't you glide slower? I can't keep up with you!"

"You ought to learn to glide," said the ghost, languidly. "It's ever so much easier than walking."

"When I'm all turned into faded smoke," said the gnome, a little crossly, "I'll try it; but I can't possibly do it now."

So the ghost glided more slowly, and the two soon came to the cottage of a wizard and a witch, who lived near the foot of the hill, where they sometimes got odd jobs from the people, who were going up to the magician's castle. As the wizard and his wife were still up, the gnome and his companion went in to see them and have a chat.

"How are you getting on?" said the ghost, as they all sat around the fire. "Have you done much incanting lately?"

"Not much," said the wizard. "We thought we would get a good deal of business when the old man died; but the folks seem to go up to the castle the same as ever."

"Yes," said the gnome, "and there's rare work going on up there now. They're trying to make root-beer for an old woman, and you never saw such a lot of poisonous trash as they have stewed up."

"They can't make root-beer!" sharply cried the witch. "They don't know anything about it. There is only one person who has the secret, and that one is myself."

"Oh, tell it to me!" exclaimed the gnome, jumping from his chair. "There's to be a reward for the person who can do it right, and——"

"Reward!" cried the witch. "Then I'm likely to tell it to you, indeed! When you're all done trying, I'm going to get that reward myself."

"Then I suppose we might as well bid you goodnight," said the gnome, and he and the ghost took their departure.

"I'll tell you what it is," said the latter, wisely shaking his head, "those people will never prosper; they're too stingy."

"True," said the gnome, and just at that moment they met a pigwidgeon, who had been sent from the castle a day or two before on a long errand. He, of course, wanted to know where the gnome and the ghost were going; but when he heard their story, he said nothing, but kept on his way.

When he reached the castle, he found that all the beer had been made, and that the busy workers had just brought out the various pots and jars into the court-yard to cool. The pigwidgeon took a sniff or two at the strange stuff in some of the jars, and then he told about the gnome and the ghost running away. When he mentioned the reason of their sudden departure, the whole assemblage stood and looked at each other in dismay.

"I never thought of that," said a tall giant; "but it's just what will happen. We shall have to taste those mixtures, and I shouldn't wonder a bit if half of them turned out to be poison. I'm going!" And so saying, he clapped on his hat, and made one step right over the court-yard wall. In an instant, every giant, genie, dwarf, fairy, gnome, afrit, elf, and the rest of them followed him out of the gate or over the wall, and swarming down the hill, they disappeared toward all quarters of the compass.

All but one young hobgoblin. He had a faithful heart, and he would not desert his mistress. He stayed behind, and in the morning, when she came down, he told her what had happened.

"And they have all deserted me," she said, sadly, "but you."

The hobgoblin bowed his head. His head was a

great deal too large, and his legs and arms were dangly, but he had an honest face.

"Perhaps they were wise," she said, looking into the pots and jars. "It might have killed them. But they were cowards to run away, instead of telling me about it; and I shall make you Ruler of the Household, because you are the only faithful one."

The hobgoblin was overwhelmed with gratitude, and could scarcely say a word.

"But I can never get along without any of them," said Filamina. "We must go and look for them; some may not be far away. We will lock the gate and take the key. May I call you Hob?"

The hobgoblin said she certainly might, if she'd like it.

"Well, then, Hob," said she, "you must go and get a chair, for we can't reach the big lock from the ground."

So Hob ran and got a chair, and brought it outside. They pulled the gate shut, and, standing on the chair, and both using all their force, they turned the big key, which the hobgoblin then took out, and carried, as they both walked away.

"You ought to be careful of the key," said Filamina, "for, if you lose it, we shall not be able to get back. Haven't you a pocket?"

"Not one big enough," said the hobgoblin: "but you might slip it down my back. It would be safe there."

So Filamina took the key and slipped it down his back. It was so big that it reached along the whole of his spine, and it was very cold; but he said never a word.

They soon came to the cottage of the wizard, and there they stopped, to ask if anything had been seen of the runaways. The witch and the wizard received them very politely, and said that they had seen a gnome and a ghost, but no others. Then Filamina told how her whole household, with the exception of the faithful hobgoblin, had gone off and deserted her; and, when she had finished her story, the witch had become very much excited. Drawing her husband to one side, she said to him:

"Engage our visitors in conversation for a time. I will be back directly."

So saying, she went into a little back-room, jumped out of the window, and ran as fast as she could to the castle.

"Just to think of it!" she said to herself, as she hurried along, "That whole castle empty! Not a creature in it! Such a chance will never happen again! I can rummage among all the wonderful treasures of the old magician. I shall learn more than I ever knew in my life!"

In the meantime, the wizard, who was a very kindly person, talked to Filamina and the hobgoblin about the wonders of Nature, and told them of his travels in various parts of the earth, all of which interested Filamina very much; and, as the hobgoblin was ever faithful to his mistress, he became just as much interested as he could be.

When the witch reached the castle, she was surprised to find the great gate locked. She had never thought of that. "I didn't see either of them have the key," she said to herself, "and it is too big to put in anybody's pocket. Perhaps they've hidden it under the step."

So she got down on her knees, and groped about under the great stone before the gate. But she found no key. Then she saw the chair which had been left by the gate.

"Oho!" she cried. "That's it! They put the key on

the ledge over the gate, and had the chair to stand on!"

She then quickly set the chair before the gate and stood up on it. But she could not yet reach the ledge, so she got up on the back. She could now barely put her hands over the ledge, and while she was feeling for the key, the chair toppled and fell over, leaving her hanging by her hands. She was afraid to drop, for she thought she would hurt herself, and so she hung, kicking and calling for help.

Just then, there came a hippogriff, who had become penitent, and determined to return to his duty. He was amazed to see the witch hanging in front of the gate, and ran up to her.

"Aha!" he cried. "Trying to climb into our castle, are you? You're a pretty one!"

"Oh, Mr. Hippogriff," said the witch, "I can explain it all to you, if I can only get down. Please put that chair under me. I'll do anything for you, if you will."

The hippogriff reflected. What could she do for him? Then he thought that perhaps she knew how to make good root-beer. So he said he would help her down if she would tell him how to make rootbeer.

"Never!" she cried. "I am going to get the reward for that myself. Anything but that!"

"Nothing but that will suit me," said the hippogriff, "and if you don't choose to tell me, I'll leave you hanging there until the giants and the afrits come back, and then you will see what you will get."

This frightened the witch very much, and in a few moments she told the hippogriff that, if he would stretch up his long neck, she would whisper the secret in his ear. So he stretched up his neck, and she told him the secret.

As soon as he had heard it, he put the chair under her, and she got down, and ran home as fast as she could go.

She reached the cottage none too soon, for the wizard was finding it very hard to keep on engaging his visitors in conversation.

Filamina now rose to go, but the witch asked her to stay a little longer.

"I suppose you know all about your good father's business," said she, "now that you are carrying it on alone?"

"No," said Filamina, "I don't understand it very well; but I try to do the best that I can."

"What you ought to do," said the witch, "is to try to find one or two persons who understand the profession of magic, and have been, perhaps, carrying it on, in a small way, themselves. Then they could do all the necessary magical work, and you would be relieved of the trouble and worry."

"That would be very nice," said Filamina, "if I could find such persons."

Just then a splendid idea came into the head of the hobgoblin. Leaning toward his mistress, he whispered, "How would these two do?"

"Good!" said Filamina, and turning to the worthy couple, she said, "Would you be willing to take the situation, and come to the castle to live?"

The witch and the wizard both said that they would be perfectly willing to do so. They would shut up their cottage, and come with her immediately, if that would please her. Filamina thought that would suit exactly, and so the cottage was shut up, and the four walked up to the castle, the witch assuring Filamina that she and her husband would find out where the runaways were, as soon as they could get to work with the magical instruments.

When they reached the gate, and Filamina pulled the key from the hobgoblin's back, the witch opened her eyes very wide.

"If I had known that," she said to herself, "I need not have lost the reward."

All now entered the castle, and the penitent hippogriff, who had been lying in a shadow of the wall, quietly followed them.

The wizard and the witch went immediately into the Dim-lit Vault, and began with great delight to examine the magical instruments. In a short time the wizard came hurrying to call Filamina.

"Here," he said, when he had brought her into the room, "is a myth-summoner. With this, you can bring back all your servants. You see these rows of keys, of so many colors. Some are for fairies, some for giants, some for genii, and there are some for each kind of creature. Strike them, and you will see what will happen."

Filamina immediately sat down before the keyboard of this strange machine, and ran her fingers along the rows of keys. In a moment, from all directions, through the air, and over the earth, came giants, fairies, afrits, genii, dwarfs, gnomes, and all the rest of them. They did not wish to come, but there was nothing for them but instant obedience when the magic keys were struck which summoned them.

They collected in the court-yard, and Filamina stood in the door-way and surveyed them.

"Don't you all feel ashamed of yourselves?" she said.

No one answered, but all hung their heads. Some

of the giants, great awkward fellows, blushed a little, and even the ghost seemed ill at ease.

"You needn't be afraid of the beer now," she said, "I am going to have it all thrown away; and you needn't have been afraid of it before. If any of you had been taken sick, we would have stopped the tasting. As you all deserted me, except this good hobgoblin, I make him Ruler of the Household, and you are to obey him. Do you understand that?"

All bowed their heads, and she left them to their own reflections.

"The next time they run away," said the faithful Hob, "you can bring them back before they go."

In a day or two, the messengers which Filamina had sent out to look for the lost rubies, and the lost lover, to inquire into the reason why the general lost his battles, and to try and find out how horseshoes could be changed into gold, returned and made their reports. They had not been recalled by the myth-summoner, because their special business, in some magical manner, disconnected them from the machine.

The gnomes who had been sent to look for the rubies, reported that they had searched everywhere, but could not find two quarts of rubies, the size of cherries. They thought the merchant must have made a mistake, and that he should have said currants. The dwarfs, who had endeavored to make gold out of horseshoes, simply stated that they could not do it; they had tried every possible method. The genie who had gone to find out why the general always lost his battles reported that his army was so much smaller and weaker than those of the neighboring countries that it was impossible for him to make a good fight; and the fairies who had searched for the lost lover said that there were very few persons, indeed, who answered to the description given by the beautiful damsel, and these were all married and settled.

Filamina, with the witch and the wizard, carefully considered these reports, and determined upon the answers to be given to the applicants when they returned.

The next day, there rode into the court-yard of the castle a high-born boy. He was somewhat startled by the strange creatures he saw around him, but he was a brave fellow, and kept steadily on until he reached the castle door, where he dismounted and entered. He was very much disappointed when he heard that the great magician was dead, for he came to consult him on an important matter.

When he saw Filamina, he told her his story. He was the son of a prince, but his father and mother had been dead for some time. Many of the people of the principality to which he was heir urged him to take his seat upon the throne, because they had been so long without a regular ruler; while another large party thought it would be much wiser for him to continue his education until he was grown up, when he would be well prepared to enter upon the duties of his high position. He had been talked to a great deal by the leaders of each of these parties, and, not being able to make up his mind as to what he should do, he had come here for advice.

"Is the country pretty well ruled now?" asked Filamina, after considering the matter a moment.

"Oh, yes," answered the high-born boy; "there are persons, appointed by my father, who govern everything all right. It's only the name of the thing that makes some of the people discontented. All the principalities in our neighborhood have regular princes, and they want one, too."

"I'll tell you what I would do," said Filamina. "I would just keep on going to school, and being taught things, until I was grown up, and knew everything that a prince ought to know. Then you could manage your principality in your own way. Look at me! Here am I with a great castle, and a whole lot of strange creatures for servants, and people coming to know things, and I can do hardly anything myself, and have to get a wizard and a witch to come and manage my business for me. I'm sure I wouldn't get into the same kind of a fix if I were you."

"I don't believe," said the high-born boy, "that I could have had any better advice than that from the very oldest magician in the world. I will do just what you have said."

Filamina now took her young visitor around the castle to show him the curious things and when he heard of the people who were coming the next day, to know what had been done for them, he agreed to stay and see how matters would turn out. Filamina's accounts had made him very much interested in the various cases.

At the appointed time, all the persons who had applied for magical assistance and information assembled in the Dim-lit Vault. Filamina sat at the end of the table, the high-born boy had a seat at her right, while the witch and the wizard were at her left. The applicants stood at the other end of the table, while the giants, afrits, and the rest of the strange household grouped themselves around the room.

"Some of these cases," said Filamina, "I have settled myself, and the others I have handed over to these wise persons, who are a wizard and a witch. They can attend to their patients first."

The high-born boy thought that she ought to have

said "clients," or "patrons," but he was too polite to speak of it.

The wizard now addressed the merchant who had lost the rubies.

"How do you know that you lost two quarts of rubies?" said he.

"I know it," replied the merchant, "because I measured them in two quart pots."

"Did you ever use those pots for anything else?" asked the wizard.

"Yes," said the merchant; "I afterward measured six quarts of sapphires with them."

"Where did you put your sapphires when you had measured them?"

"I poured them into a peck jar," said the merchant.

"Did they fill it?" asked the wizard.

"Yes; I remember thinking that I might as well tie a cloth over the top of the jar, for it would hold no more."

"Well, then," said the wizard, "as six quarts of sapphires will not fill a peck jar, I think you will find your rubies at the bottom of the jar, where you probably poured them when you wished to use the quart pots for the sapphires."

"I shouldn't wonder," said the merchant. "I'll go right home and see."

He went home, and sure enough, under the six quarts of sapphires, he found his rubies.

"As for you," said the wizard to the general who always lost his battles, "your case is very simple: your army is too weak. What you want is about twelve giants, and this good young lady says she is willing to furnish them. Twelve giants, well armed with iron clubs, tremendous swords and long spears, with which they could reach over moats and walls, and poke the enemy, would make your army almost irresistible."

"Oh, yes," said the general, looking very much troubled, "that is all true; but think how much it would cost to keep a dozen enormous giants! They would eat more than all the rest of the army. My king is poor; he is not able to support twelve giants."

"In that case," said the wizard, "war is a luxury which he cannot afford. If he cannot provide the means to do his fighting in the proper way, he ought to give it up, and you and he should employ your army in some other way. Set the soldiers at some profitable work, and then the kingdom will not be so poor."

The general could not help thinking that this was very good advice, and when he went home and told his story, his king agreed with him. The kingdom lay between two seas, and the soldiers were set to work to cut a canal right though the middle of the country, from one sea to the other.

Then the ships belonging to the neighboring kingdoms were allowed to sail through this canal, and charged a heavy toll. In this way the kingdom became very prosperous, and everybody agreed that it was a great deal better than carrying on wars and always being beaten.

The wizard next spoke to the young man who wanted to know how to make gold out of horseshoes.

"I think you will have to give up your idea," he declared. "The best metal-workers here have failed in the undertaking, and I myself have tried, for many years, to turn old iron into gold, but never could do it. Indeed, it is one of the things which magicians cannot do. Are you so poor that you are much in need of gold?"

"Oh, no," said the young man. "I am not poor at all. But I would like very much to be able to make gold whenever I please."

"The best thing you can do," said the wizard, "if you really wish to work in metals, is to make horseshoes out of gold. This will be easier than the other plan, and will not worry your mind so much."

The young man stood aside. He did not say anything, but he looked very much disappointed.

This ended the wizard's cases, and Filamina now began to do her part. She first called up the greedy king who wanted the adjoining kingdom.

"Here is a bottle," she said, "which contains a very bad disease, for an old person and a very bad one for a child. Whenever you feel that you would like the old king and the young heir, who stand between you and the kingdom you want, to be sick, take a good drink from the bottle."

The greedy king snatched the bottle, and, as soon as he reached home, he took a good drink, and he had the rheumatism and the colic so bad that he never again wished to make anybody sick.

"As for you," said Filamina to the beautiful damsel who had lost her lover, "my fairy messengers have not been able to find any person, such as you describe, who is not married and settled. So your lover must have married some one else. And, as you cannot get him, I think the best thing you can do is to marry this young man, who wanted to make horseshoes into gold. Of course, neither of you will get exactly what you came for, but it will be better than going away without anything."

The beautiful damsel and the young man stepped aside and talked the matter over, and they soon agreed to Filamina's plan, and went away quite happy.

"I am dreadfully sorry," said Filamina to the old woman who wanted to know how to make a good root-beer, and who sat in the sedan-chair which had been sent for her, "but we have tried our best to find out how to make good root-beer, and the stuff we brewed was awful. I have asked this learned witch about it, and she says she does not now possess the secret. I have also offered a reward to any one who can tell me how to do it, but no one seems to want to try for it."

At this moment, the penitent hippogriff came forward from a dark corner where he had been sitting, and said: "I know what you must use to make good root-beer."

"What is it?" asked Filamina.

"Roots," said the hippogriff.

"That's perfectly correct," said the witch. "If a person will use roots, instead of all sorts of drugs and strange decoctions, they will make root-beer that is really good."

A great joy crept over the face of the old woman, and again and again she thanked Filamina for this precious secret.

The two giants raised her in the sedan-chair, and bore her away to her home, where she immediately set to work to brew root-beer from roots. Her beer soon became so popular that she was enabled to support her sons and daughters in luxury, and to give each of her grandchildren an excellent education.

When all the business was finished, and the penitent hippogriff had been given his reward, Filamina said to the high-born boy:

"Now it is all over, and everybody has had something done for him or for her."

"No," said the other, "I do not think so. Nothing has been done for you. You ought not to be left here alone with all these creatures. You may be used to them, but I think they're horrible. You gave me some advice which was very good, and now I am going to give you some, which perhaps you may like. I think you ought to allow this wizard and this witch, who seem like very honest people, to stay here and carry on the business. Then you could leave this place, and go to school, and learn all the things that girls know who don't live in old magical castles. After a while, when you are grown up, and I am grown up, we could be married, and we could both rule over my principality. What do you think of that plan?"

"I think it would be very nice," said Filamina, "and I really believe I will do it."

It was exactly what she did do. The next morning, her white horse was brought from the castle stables, and side by side, and amid the cheers and farewells of the giants, the dwarfs, the gnomes, the fairies, the afrits, the genii, the pigwidgeons, the witch, the wizard, the ghosts, the penitent hippogriff, and the faithful hobgoblin, Filamina and the high-born boy rode away to school.

Ting-a-ling

I N A far country of the East, in a palace surrounded by orange groves, where the nightingales sang, and by silvery lakes, where the soft
fountains plashed, there lived a fine old king. For
many years he had governed with great comfort to
himself, and to the tolerable satisfaction of his subjects. His queen being dead, his whole affection was
given to his only child, the Princess Aufalia; and,
whenever he happened to think of it, he paid great
attention to her education. She had the best masters
of embroidery and in the language of flowers, and
she took lessons on the zithar three times a week.

A suitable husband, the son of a neighboring
monarch, had been selected for her when she was
about two hours old, thus making it unnecessary for
her to go into society, and she consequently passed
her youthful days in almost entire seclusion. She
was now, when our story begins, a woman more

beautiful than the roses of the garden, more musical than the nightingales, and far more graceful than the plashing fountain.

One balmy day in spring, when the birds were singing lively songs on the trees, and the crocuses were coaxing the jonquils almost off their very stems with their pretty ways, Aufalia went out to take a little promenade, followed by two grim slaves. Closely veiled, she walked in the secluded suburbs of the town, where she was generally required to take her lonely exercise. To-day, however, the slaves, impelled by a sweet tooth, which each of them possessed, thought it would be no harm if they went a little out of their way to procure some sugared cream-beans, which were made excellently well by a confectioner near the outskirts of the city. While they were in the shop, bargaining for the sugar-beans, a young man who was passing thereby stepped up to the Princess, and asked her if she could tell him the shortest road to the baths, and if there was a good eating-house in the neighborhood. Now as this was the first time in her life that the Princess had been addressed by a young man, it is not surprising that she was too much astonished to speak, especially as this youth was well dressed, extremely handsome, and of proud and dignified manners,—although, to be sure, a little travel-stained and tired-looking.

When she had somewhat recovered from her embarrassment, she raised her veil, (as if it was necessary to do so in speaking to a young man!) and told him that she was sure she had not the slightest idea where any place in the city was,—that she very seldom went into the city, and never thought about the way to any place when she did go,—that she wished she knew where those places were that he mentioned, for she would very much like to tell him, especially if he was hungry, which she knew was not pleasant, and no doubt he was not used to it, but that indeed she hadn't any idea about the way anywhere, but—

There is no knowing how long the Princess might have run on thus (and her veil up all the time) had not the two slaves at that moment emerged from the sugar-bean shop. The sight of the Princess actually talking to a young man in the broad daylight so amazed them, that they stood for a moment dumb in the door. But, recovering from their surprise, they drew their cimeters, and ran toward the Prince (for such his every action proclaimed him to be). When this high-born personage saw them coming with drawn blades, his countenance flushed, and his eyes sparkled with rage. Drawing his flashing sword, he shouted, "Crouch, varlets! Lie with the dust, ye dogs!" and sprang furiously upon them.

The impetuosity of the onslaught caused the two men to pause, and in a few minutes they fell back some yards, so fast and heavy did the long sword clash upon their upraised cimeters. This contest was soon over, for, unaccustomed to such a vigorous method of attack, the slaves turned and fled, and the Prince pursued them down a long street, and up an alley, and over a wall, and through a garden, and under an arch, and over a court-yard, and through a gate, and down another street, and up another alley, and through a house, and up a long staircase, and out upon a roof, and over several abutments, and down a trap-door, and down another pair of stairs, and through another house, into another garden, and over another wall, and down a long road, and over a field, clear out of sight.

When the Prince had performed this feat, he sat

down to rest, but, suddenly bethinking himself of the maiden, he rose and went to look for her.

"I have chased away her servants," said he; "how will she ever find her way anywhere?"

If this was difficult for her, the Prince found that it was no less so for himself; and he spent much time in endeavoring to reach again the northern suburbs of the city. At last, after considerable walking, he reached the long street into which he had first chased the slaves, and, finding a line of children eagerly devouring a line of sugared cream-beans, he remembered seeing these confections dropping from the pockets of the slaves as he pursued them, and, following up the clew, soon reached the shop, and found the Princess sitting under a tree before the door. The shop-keeper, knowing her to be the Princess, had been afraid to speak to her, and was working away inside, making believe that he had not seen her, and that he knew nothing of the conflict which had taken place before his door.

Up jumped Aufalia. "O! I am so glad to see you again! I have been waiting here ever so long. But what have you done with my slaves?"

"I am your slave," said the Prince, bowing to the ground.

"But you don't know the way home," said she, "and I am dreadfully hungry."

Having ascertained from her that she was the King's daughter, and lived at the palace, the Prince reflected for a moment, and then, entering the shop, dragged forth the maker of sugared cream-beans, and ordered him to lead the way to the presence of the King. The confectioner, crouching to the earth, immediately started off, and the Prince and Princess, side by side, followed over what seemed to them a very short road to the palace. The Princess talked a great deal, but the Prince was rather quiet. He had a good many things to think about. He was the younger son of a king who lived far away to the north, and had been obliged to flee the kingdom on account of the custom of allowing only one full-grown heir to the throne to live in the country.

"Now," thought he, "this is an excellent commencement of my adventures. Here is a truly lovely Princess whom I am conducting to her anxious parent. He will be overwhelmed with gratitude, and will doubtless bestow upon me the government of a province—or—perhaps he will make me his Vizier—no, I will not accept that,—the province will suit me better." Having settled this little matter to his mind, he gladdened the heart of the Princess with the dulcet tones of his gentle voice.

On reaching the palace, they went directly to the grand hall, where the King was giving audience. Justly astounded at perceiving his daughter (now veiled) approaching under the guidance of a crouching sugar-bean maker and a strange young man, he sat in silent amazement, until the Prince, who was used to court life, had made his manners, and related his story. When the King had heard it, he clapped his hands three times, and in rushed twenty-four eunuchs.

"Take," said the monarch, "this bird to her bower." And they surrounded the Princess, and hurried her off to the women's apartments.

Then he clapped his hands twice, and in rushed twenty-four armed guards from another door.

"Bind me this dog!" quoth the King, pointing to the Prince. And they bound him in a twinkling.

"Is this the way you treat a stranger?" cried the Prince.

"Aye," said the King, merrily. "We will treat you

royally. You are tired. To-night and to-morrow you shall be lodged and feasted daintily and the day after we will have a celebration, when you shall be beaten with sticks, and shall fight a tiger, and be tossed by a bull, and be bowstrung, and beheaded, and drawn and quartered, and we will have a nice time. Bear him away to his soft couch."

The guards then led the Prince away to be kept a prisoner until the day for the celebration. The room to which he was conducted was comfortable, and he soon had a plenteous supper laid out before him, of which he partook with great avidity. Having finished his meal, he sat down to reflect upon his condition, but feeling very sleepy, and remembering that he would have a whole day of leisure, to-morrow, for such reflections, he concluded to go to bed. Before doing so, however, he wished to make all secure for the night. Examining the door, he found there was no lock to it; and being unwilling to remain all night liable to intrusion, he pondered the matter for some minutes, and then took up a wide and very heavy stool, and, having partially opened the door, he put the stool up over it, resting it partly on the door and partly on the surrounding woodwork, so that if any one tried to come in, and pushed the door open, the stool would fall down and knock the intruder's head off. Having arranged this to his satisfaction, the Prince went to bed.

That evening the Princess Aufalia was in great grief, for she had heard of the sentence pronounced upon the Prince, and felt herself the cause of it. What other reason she had to grieve over the Prince's death, need not be told. Her handmaidens fully sympathized with her; and one of them, Nerralina, the handsomest and most energetic of them all, soon found, by proper inquiry, that the Prince was confined in the fourth story of the "Tower of Tears." So they devised a scheme for his rescue. Each one of the young ladies contributed her scarf; and when they were all tied together, the conclave decided that they made a rope plenty long enough to reach from the Prince's window to the ground.

Thus much settled, it only remained to get this means of escape to the prisoner. This the lady Nerralina volunteered to do. Waiting until the dead of night, she took off her slippers, and with the scarf-rope rolled up into a ball under her arm, she silently stepped past the drowsy sentinels, and, reaching the Prince's room, pushed open the door, and the stool fell down and knocked her head off. Her body lay in the doorway, but her head rolled into the middle of the room.

Notwithstanding the noise occasioned by this accident, the Prince did not awake; but in the morning, when he was up and nearly dressed, he was astonished at seeing a lady's head in the middle of the room.

"Hallo!" said he. "Here's somebody's head."

Picking it up, he regarded it with considerable interest. Then seeing the body in the doorway, he put the head and it together, and, finding they fitted, came to the conclusion that they belonged to each other, and that the stool had done the mischief. When he saw the bundle of scarfs lying by the body, he unrolled it, and soon imagined the cause of the lady's visit.

"Poor thing!" he said; "doubtless the Princess sent her here with this, and most likely with a message also, which now I shall never hear. But these poor women! what do they know! This rope will not bear a man like me. Well! well! this poor girl is dead. I will pay respect to her."

And so he picked her up, and put her on his bed, thinking at the time that she must have fainted when she heard the stool coming, for no blood had flowed. He fitted on the head, and then he covered her up with the sheet; but, in pulling this over her head, he uncovered her feet, which he now perceived to be slipperless.

"No shoes! Ah me! Well, I will be polite to a lady, even if she is dead."

And so he drew off his own yellow boots, and put them on her feet, which was easy enough, as they were a little too big for her. He had hardly done this, and dressed himself, when he heard some one approaching; and hastily removing the fallen stool, he got behind the door just as a fat old fellow entered with a broadsword in one hand, and a pitcher of hot water and some towels in the other. Glancing at the bed, and seeing the yellow boots sticking out, the old fellow muttered: "Gone to bed with his clothes on, eh? Well, I'll let him sleep!" And so, putting down the pitcher and the towels, he walked out again. But not alone, for the Prince silently stepped after him, and by keeping close behind him, followed without being heard,—his politeness having been the fortunate cause of his being in his stocking-feet. For some distance they walked together thus, the Prince intending to slip off at the first cross passage he came to. It was quite dusky in the long hall way, there being no windows; and when the guard, at a certain place, made a very wide step, taking hold of a rod by the side of the wall as he did so, the Prince, not perceiving this, walked straight on, and popped right down an open trap-door.

Nerralina not returning, the Princess was in great grief, not knowing at first whether she had eloped with the Prince, or had met with some misfortune on the way to his room. In the morning, however, the ladies ascertained that the rope was not hanging from the Prince's window; and as the guards reported that he was comfortably sleeping in his bed, it was unanimously concluded that Nerralina had been discovered in her attempt, and had come to grief. Sorrowing bitterly, somewhat for the unknown mishap of her maid of honor, but still more for the now certain fate of him she loved, Aufalia went into the garden, and, making her way through masses of rose trees and jasmines, to the most secluded part of the grounds, threw herself upon a violet bank and wept unrestrainedly, the tears rolling one by one from her eyes, like a continuous string of pearls.

Now it so happened that this spot was the pleasure ground of a company of fairies, who had a colony near by. These fairies were about an inch and a half high, beautifully formed, and of the most respectable class. They had not been molested for years by any one coming to this spot; but as they knew perfectly well who the Princess was, they were not at all alarmed at her appearance. In fact, the sight of her tears rolling so prettily down into the violet cups, and over the green leaves, seemed to please them much, and many of the younger ones took up a tear or two upon their shoulders to take home with them.

There was one youth, the handsomest of them all, named Ting-a-ling, who had a beautiful little sweetheart called Ling-a-ting.

Each one of these lovers, when they were about to return to their homes, picked up the prettiest tear they could find. Ting-a-ling put his tear upon his shoulder, and walked along as gracefully as an Egyptian woman with her water-jug; while little Ling-a-ting, with her treasure borne lightly over her head, skipped by her lover's side, as happy as happy could be.

"Don't walk out in the sun, my dearest," said Ting-a-ling. "Your shin-shiney will burst."

"Burst! O no, Tingy darling, no it won't. See how nice and big it is getting, and so light! Look!" cried she, throwing back her head; "I can see the sky through it; and O! what pretty colors,—blue, green, pink, and"—And the tear burst, and poor little Ling-a-ting sunk down on the grass, drenched and drowned.

Horror-stricken, Ting-a-ling dropped his tear and wept. Clasping his hands above his head, he fell on his knees beside his dear one, and raised his eyes to the blue sky in bitter anguish. But when he cast them down again, little Ling-a-ting was all soaked into the grass. Then sterner feelings filled his breast, and revenge stirred up the depths of his soul.

"This thing shall end!" he said, hissing the words between his teeth. "No more of us shall die like Ling-a-ting!"

So he ran quickly, and with his little sword cut down two violets, and of the petals he made two little soft bundles, and, tying them together with his garters, he slung them over his shoulder. Full of his terrible purpose, he then ran to the Princess, and, going behind her, clambered up her dress until he stood on her shoulder, and, getting on the top of her head, he loosened a long hair, and lowered himself down with it, until he stood upon the under lashes of her left eye. Now, his intention was evident. Those violet bundles were to "end this thing." They were to be crammed into the source of those fatal tears, to the beauty of which poor Ling-a-ting had fallen a victim.

"Now we shall see," said he, "if some things cannot be done as well as others!" and, kneeling down, he took one bundle from his shoulder, and prepared to put it in her eye. It is true, that, occupying the position he did, he, in some measure, obstructed the lady's vision; but as her eyes had been so long dimmed with tears, and her heart over-shadowed with sorrow, she did not notice it.

Just as Ting-a-ling was about to execute his purpose, he happened to look before him, and saw, to his amazement, another little fairy on his knees, right in front of him. Starting back, he dropped the bundle from his hand, and the other from his shoulder. Then, upon his hands and knees, he stared steadfastly at the little man opposite to him, who immediately imitated him. And there they knelt with equal wonder in each of their countenances, bobbing at each other every time the lady winked. Then did Ting-a-ling get very red in the face, and, standing erect, he took strong hold of the Princess's upper eyelash, to steady himself, resolved upon giving that saucy fairy a good kick, when, to his dismay, the eyelash came out, he lost his balance, and at the same moment a fresh shower of tears burst from her eyes, which washed Ting-a-ling senseless into her lap.

When he recovered, he was still sticking to the Princess's silk apron, all unobserved, as she sat in her own room talking to one of her maids, who had just returned from a long visit into the country. Slipping down to the floor, Ting-a-ling ran all shivering to the window, to the seat of which he climbed, and getting upon a chrysanthemum that was growing in a flower-pot in the sunshine, he took off his shoes and stockings, and, hanging them on a branch to dry, lay down in the warm blossom; and while he was drying, listened to the mournful tale that Aufalia was telling her maid, about the poor Prince that was to die to-morrow. The more he heard, the more was his tender heart touched with pity, and, forgetting all his resentment against the Princess, he felt only the deepest sympathy for her misfortunes, and those of her lover. When she had finished, Ting-a-ling had resolved to assist them, or die in the attempt!

But, as he could not do much himself, he intended instantly to lay their case before a Giant of his acquaintance, whose good-humor and benevolence were proverbial. So he put on his shoes and stockings, which were not quite dry, and hastily descended to the garden by means of a vine which grew upon the wall. The distance to the Giant's castle was too great for him to think of walking; and he hurried around to a friend of his who kept a livery-stable. When he reached this place, he found his friend sitting in his stable-door, and behind him Ting-a-ling could see the long rows of stalls, with all the butterflies on one side, and the grasshoppers on the other.

"How do you do?" said Ting-a-ling, seating himself upon a horse-block, and wiping his face. "It is a hot day, isn't it?"

"Yes, sir," said the livery-stable man, who was rounder and shorter than Ting-a-ling. "Yes, it is very warm. I haven't been out to-day."

"Well, I shouldn't advise you to go," said Ting-a-ling. "But I must to business, for I'm in a great hurry. Have you a fast butterfly that you can let me have right away?"

"O yes, two or three of them, for that matter."

"Have you that one," asked Ting-a-ling, "that I used to take out last summer?"

"That animal," said the livery-stable man, rising and clasping his hands under his coat-tail, "I am sorry to say, you can't have. He's foundered."

"That's bad," said Ting-a-ling, "for I always liked him."

"I can let you have one just as fast," said the stablekeeper. "By the way, how would you like a real good grasshopper?"

"Too hot a day for the saddle," said Ting-a-ling; "and now please harness up, for I'm in a dreadful hurry."

"Yes, sir, right away. But I don't know exactly what wagon to give you. I have two first-rate new pea-pods; but they are both out. However, I can let you have a nice easy Johnny-jump-up, if you say so."

"Any thing will do," said Ting-a-ling, "only get it out quick."

In a very short time a butterfly was brought out, and harnessed to a first-class Johnny-jump-up. The vehicles used by these fairies were generally a cup-like blossom, or something of that nature, furnished, instead of wheels, with little bags filled with a gas resembling that used to inflate balloons. Thus the vehicle was sustained in the air, while the steed drew it rapidly along.

As soon as Ting-a-ling heard the sound of the approaching equipage, he stood upon the horse-block, and when the wagon was brought up to it, he quickly jumped in and took the reins from the hostler. "Get up!" said he, and away they went.

It was a long drive, and it was at least three in the afternoon when Ting-a-ling reached the Giant's castle. Drawing up before the great gates, he tied his animal to a hinge, and walked in himself under the gate. Going boldly into the hall, he went up-stairs, or rather he ran up the top rail of the banisters, for it would have been hard work for him to have clambered up each separate step. As he expected, he found the Giant (whose name I forgot to say was Tur-il-i-ra) in his dining-room. He had just finished his dinner, and was sitting in his arm-chair by the table, fast asleep. This Giant was about as large as two mammoths. It was useless for Ting-a-ling to stand on the floor, and endeavor to make himself heard above the roaring of the snoring, which sounded louder than the thunders of a cataract. So, climbing upon one of the Giant's boots, he ran up his leg, and hurried over the waistcoat so fast, that, slipping on one of the brass buttons, he came down upon his knees with great force.

"Whew!" said he, "that must have hurt him! after dinner too!"

Jumping up quickly, he ran easily over the bosom, and getting on his shoulder, clambered up into his ear. Standing up in the opening of this immense cavity, he took hold of one side with his outstretched arms, and shouted with all his might,—

"*Tur*-il-i! *Tur*-il-i! *Tur*-il-i-RA!"

Startled at the noise, the Giant clapped his hand to his ear with such force, that had not Ting-a-ling held on very tightly, he would have been shot up against the tympanum of this mighty man.

"Don't do that again!" cried the little fellow. "Don't do that again! It's only me—Ting-a-ling. Hold your finger."

Recognizing the voice of his young friend, the Giant held out his forefinger, and Ting-a-ling, mounting it, was carried round before the Giant's face, where he proceeded to relate the misfortunes of the two lovers, in his most polished and affecting style.

The Giant listened with much attention, and when he had done, said, "Ting-a-ling, I feel a great interest in all young people, and will do what I can for this truly unfortunate couple. But I must finish my nap first, otherwise I could not do anything. Please jump down on the table and eat something, while I go to sleep for a little while."

So saying, he put Ting-a-ling gently down upon the table. But this young gentleman, having a dainty appetite, did not see much that he thought he would like; but, cutting a grain of rice in two, he ate the half of it, and then lay down on a napkin and went to sleep.

When Tur-il-i-ra awoke, he remembered that it was time to be off, and, waking Ting-a-ling, he took out his great purse, and placed the little fairy in it, where he had very comfortable quarters, as there was no money there to hurt him.

"Don't forget my wagon when you get to the gate," said Ting-a-ling, sleepily, rolling himself up for a fresh nap, as the Giant closed the purse with a snap. Tur-il-i-ra, having put on his hat, went downstairs, and crossed the court-yard in a very few steps. When he had closed the great gates after him, he bethought himself of Ting-a-ling's turn-out, which the fairy had mentioned as being tied to the hinge. Not being able to see anything so minute at the distance of his eyes from the ground, he put on his spectacles, and getting upon his hands and knees, peered closely about the hinges.

"O! here you are," said he, and, picking up the butterfly and wagon, he put them in his vest pocket—that is, all excepting the butterfly's head. That remained fast to the hinge, as the Giant forgot he was tied. Then our lofty friend set off at a smart pace for the King's castle; but notwithstanding his haste, it was dark when he reached it.

"Come now, young man," said he, opening his

purse, "wake up, and let us get to work. Where is that Prince you were talking about?"

"Well, I'm sure I don't know," said Ting-a-ling, rubbing his eyes. "But just put me up to that window which has the vine growing beneath it. That is the Princess's room, and she can tell us all about it."

So the giant took him on his finger, and put him in the window. There, in the lighted room, Ting-a-ling beheld a sight which greatly moved him. Although she had slept but little the night before, the Princess was still up, and was sitting in an easy-chair, weeping profusely. Near her stood a maid-of-honor, who continually handed her fresh handkerchiefs from a great basketful by her side. As fast as the Princess was done with one, she threw it behind her, and the great pile there showed that she must have been weeping nearly all day. Getting down upon the floor, Ting-a-ling clambered up the Princess's dress, and reaching, at last, her ear, shouted into it,—

"Princess! Princess! Stop crying, for I'm come!"

The Princess was very much startled; but she did not, like the Giant, clap her hand to her ear, for if she had, she would have ruined the beautiful curls which stood out so nicely on each side. Ting-a-ling implored her to be quiet, and told her that the Giant had come to assist her, and that they wanted to know where the Prince was confined.

"I will tell you! I will show you!" cried the Princess quickly, and, jumping up, she ran to the window with Ting-a-ling still at her ear. "O you good giant," she cried, "are you there? If you will take me, I will show you the tower, the cruel tower, where my Prince is confined."

"Fear not!" said the good Giant. "Fear not! I soon

will release him. Let me take you in my hands, and do you show me where to go."

"Are you sure you can hold me?" said the Princess, standing timidly upon the edge of the window.

"I guess so," said the Giant. "Just get into my hands."

And, taking her down gently, he set her on his arm, and then he took Ting-a-ling from her hair, and placed him on the tip of his thumb. Thus they proceeded to the Tower of Tears.

"Here is the place," said the Princess. "Here is the horrid tower where my beloved is. Please put me down a minute, and let me cry."

"No, no," said the Giant; "you have done enough of that, my dear, and we have no time to spare. So, if this is your Prince's tower, just get in at the window, and tell him to come out quickly, and I will take you both away without making any fuss."

"That is the window—the fourth-story one. Lift me up," said the Princess.

But though the Giant was very large, he was not quite tall enough for this feat, for they built their towers very high in those days. So, putting Ting-a-ling and the Princess into his pocket, he looked around for something to stand on. Seeing a barn near by, he picked it up, and placed it underneath the window. He put his foot on it to try if it would bear him, and, finding it would (for in those times barns were very strong), he stood upon it and looked in the fourth-story window. Taking his little friends out of his pocket, he put them on the window-sill, where Ting-a-ling remained to see what would happen, but the Princess jumped right down on the floor. As there was a lighted candle on the table, she saw that there was some one covered up in the bed.

"O, there he is!" said she. "Now I will wake him

up, and hurry him away." But just at that moment, as she was going to give the sleeper a gentle shake, she happened to perceive the yellow boots sticking out from under the sheet.

"O dear!" said she in a low voice, "if he hasn't gone to bed with his boots on! And if I wake him, he will jump right down on the floor, and make a great noise, and we shall be found out."

So she went to the foot of the bed, and pulled off the boots very gently.

"White stockings!" said she. "What does this mean? I know the Prince wore green stockings, for I took particular notice how well they looked with his yellow boots. There must be something wrong, I declare! Let me run to the other end of the bed, and see how it is there. O my! O my!" cried she, turning down the sheet. "A woman's head! Wrong both ways! O what shall I do?"

Letting the sheet drop, she accidentally touched the head, which immediately rolled off on to the floor.

"Loose! Loose!! Loose!!!" she screamed in bitter agony, clasping her hands above her head. "What shall I ever do? O misery! misery me! Some demon has changed him, all but his boots. O Despair! Despair!"

And, without knowing what she did, she rushed frantically out of the room, and along the dark passage, and popped right down through the open trap.

"What's up?" said the Giant, putting his face to the window. "What's all this noise about?"

"O I don't know," said Ting-a-ling, almost crying, "but somebody's head is off; and it's a lady—all but the boots—and the Princess has run away! O dear! O dear!"

"Come now!" said Tur-il-i-ra, "Ting-a-ling, get

into my pocket. I must see into this myself, for I can't be waiting here all night, you know."

So the Giant, still standing on the barn, lifted off the roof of the tower, and threw it to some distance. He then, by the moonlight, examined the upper story, but, finding no Prince or Princess, brushed down the walls until he came to the floor, and, taking it up, he looked carefully over the next story. This he continued, until he had torn down the whole tower, and found no one but servants and guards, who ran away in all directions, like ants when you destroy their hills. He then kicked down all those walls which connected the tower with the rest of the palace, and, when it was all level with the ground, he happened to notice, almost at his feet, a circular opening like an entrance to a vault, from which arose a very pleasant smell as of something good to eat. Stooping down to see what it was that caused this agreeable perfume, he perceived that at the distance of a few yards the aperture terminated in a huge yellow substance, in which, upon a closer inspection, he saw four feet sticking up—two with slippers, and two with green stockings.

"Why, this is strange!" said he, and, stooping down, he felt the substance, and found it was quite soft and yielding. He then loosened it by passing his hand around it, and directly lifted it out almost entire.

"By the beard of the Prophet!" he cried, "but this is a cheese!" and, turning it over, he saw on the other side two heads, one with short black hair, and the other covered with beautiful brown curls.

"Why, here they are! As I'm a living Giant! these must be the Prince and Princess, stowed away in a cheese!" And he laughed until the very hills cracked.

When he got a little over his merriment, he asked

the imprisoned couple how they got there, and if they felt comfortable. They replied that they had fallen down a trap, and had gone nearly through this cheese, where they had stuck fast, and that was all they had known about it; and if the blood did not run down into their heads so, they would be pretty comfortable, thank him—which last remark the Giant accounted for by the fact, that, when lovers are near each other, they do not generally pay much attention to surrounding circumstances.

"This, then," said he, rising, "is where the King hardens his cheeses, is it? Well, well, it's a jolly go!" And he laughed some more.

"O Tur-il-i-ra," cried Ting-a-ling, looking out from the vest-pocket, "I'm so glad you've found them."

"Well, so am I," said the Giant.

Then Tur-il-i-ra, still holding the cheese, walked away for a little distance, and sat down on a high bank, intending to wait there until morning, when he would call on the King, and confer with him in relation to his newfound treasure. Leaning against a great rock, the Giant put the cheese upon his knees in such a manner as not to injure the heads and feet of the lovers, and dropped into a very comfortable sleep.

"Don't I wish I could get my arms out!" whispered the Prince.

"O my!" whispered the Princess.

Ting-a-ling, having now nothing to occupy his mind, and desiring to stretch his legs, got out of the vest-pocket where he had remained so safely during all the disturbance, and descended to the ground to take a little walk. He had not gone far before he met a young friend, who was running along as fast as he could.

"Hallo! Ting-a-ling," cried the other. "Is that you?

Come with me, and I will show you the funniest thing you ever saw in your life."

"Is it far?" said Ting-a-ling, "for I must be back here by daylight."

"O no! come on. It won't take you long, and I tell you, it's fun!"

So away they ran, merrily vaulting over the hickory-nuts, or acorns, that happened to be in their way, in mere playfulness, as if they were nothing. They soon came to a large, open space, so brightly lighted by the moon, that every object was as visible as if it were daylight. Scattered over the smooth green were thousands of fairies of Ting-a-ling's nation, the most of whom were standing gazing intently at a very wonderful sight.

Seated on a stone, under a great tree that stood all alone in the center of this plain, was a woman without any head. She moved her hands rapidly about over her shoulders, as if in search of the missing portion of herself, and, encountering nothing but mere air, she got very angry, and stamped her feet, and shrugged her shoulders, which amused the fairies very much, and they all set up a great laugh, and seemed to be enjoying the fun amazingly. On one side, down by a little brook, was a busy crowd of fairies, who appeared to be washing something therein. Scattered all around were portions of the Tower of Tears, much of which had fallen hereabouts.

Ting-a-ling and his friend had not gazed long upon this scene before the sound of music was heard, and in a few moments there appeared from out the woods a gorgeous procession. First came a large band of music, ringing blue-bells and blowing honeysuckles. Then came an array of courtiers, magnificently dressed, and, after them, the Queen of the fairies, riding in a beautiful water-lily, drawn by six royal purple butterflies, and surrounded by a brilliant body of lords and ladies.

This procession halted at a short distance in front of the lady-minus-a-head, and formed itself into a semicircle, with the Queen in the centre. Then the crowd at the brook were seen approaching, and on the shoulders of the multitude was borne a head. They hurried as fast as their heavy load would permit, until they came to the tree under which sat the headless Nerralina, who, bed and all, had fallen here, when the Giant tore down the tower. Then quickly attaching a long rope (that they had put over a branch directly above the lady) to the hair of the head, they all took hold of the other end, and, pulling with a will, soon hoisted the head up until it hung at some distance above the neck to which it had previously belonged. Now they began to lower it slowly, and the Queen stood up with her wand raised ready to utter the magic word which should unite the parts when they touched. A deep silence spread over the plain, and even the lady seemed conscious that something was about to happen, for she stood up and remained perfectly still.

There was but one person there who did not feel pleasure at the approaching event, and that was a dwarf about a foot high, very ugly and wicked, who, by some means or other, had got into this goodly company, and who was now seated in a crotch of the tree, very close to the rope by which the crowd was lowering the lady's head. No one perceived him, for he was very much the color of the tree, and there he sat alone, quivering with spite and malice.

At the moment the head touched the ivory neck, the Queen, uttering the magic word, dropped the end of the wand, and immediately the head adhered as firmly as of old.

But a wild shout of horror rang through all the plain! For, at the critical moment, the dwarf had reached out his hand, and twisted the rope, so that when the head was joined, it was wrong side foremost—face back!

Just then the little villain stuck his head out from behind the branch, and, giving a loud and mocking laugh of triumph, dropped from the tree. With a yell of anger the whole crowd, Queen, courtiers, common people, and all, set off in a mad chase after the dwarf, who fled like a stag before the hounds.

All were gone but little Ting-a-ling, and when he saw the dreadful distress of poor Nerralina, who jumped up, and twisted around, and ran backward both ways, screaming for help, he stopped not a minute, but ran to where he had left the Giant, and told him, as fast as his breathing would allow, the sad story.

Rubbing his eyes, Tur-il-i-ra perceived that it was nearly day, and concluded to commence operations. He placed Ting-a-ling on his shirt-frill, where he could see what was going on, and, taking about eleven strides, he came to where poor Nerralina was jumping about, and, picking her up, put her carefully into his coat-tail pocket. Then, with the cheese in his hand, he walked slowly toward the palace.

When he arrived there, he found the people running about, and crowding around the ruins of the Tower of Tears. He passed on, however, to the great Audience Chamber, and, looking in, saw the King sitting upon his throne behind a velvet-covered table, holding an early morning council, and receiving the reports of his officers concerning the damage. As this Hall, and the doors thereof, were of great size, the Giant walked in, stooping a little as he entered.

He marched right up to the King, and held the cheese down before him.

"Here, your Majesty, is your daughter, and the young Prince, her lover. Does your Majesty recognize them?"

"Well, I declare!" cried the King. "If that isn't my great cheese, that I had put in the vault-flue to harden! And my daughter and that young man in it! What does this mean? What have you been doing, Giant?"

Then Tur-il-i-ra related the substance of the whole affair in a very brief manner, and concluded by saying that he hoped to see them made man and wife, as he considered them under his protection, and intended to see them safely through this affair. And he held them up so that all the people who thronged into the Hall could see.

The people all laughed, but the King cried "Silence!" and said to the Giant, "If the young man is of as good blood as my daughter, I have no desire to separate them. In fact, I don't think I am separating them. I think it's the cheese!"

"Come! come!" said the Giant, turning very red in the face, "none of your trifling, or I'll knock your house down over your eyes!"

And, putting the cheese down close to the table, he broke it in half, letting the lovers drop out on the velvet covering, when they immediately rushed into each other's arms, and remained thus clasped for a length of time.

They then slowly relinquished their hold upon each other, and were exchanging looks of supreme tenderness, when the Prince, happening to glance at his feet, sprang back so that he almost fell off the long table, and shouted,—

"Blood! Fire! Thunder! Where's my boots? Boots! Slaves! Hounds! Get me my boots! boots!! boots!!!"

"O! he's a Prince!" cried the King, jumping up. "I want no further proof. He's a Prince. Give him boots. And blow, horners, blow! Beat your drums, drummers! Join hands all! Clear the floor for a dance!"

And in a trice the floor was cleared, and about five thousand couples stood ready for the first note from the band.

"Hold up!" cried the Giant. "Hold up! here is one I forgot," and he commenced feeling in his pockets. "I know I have got her somewhere. O yes, here she is!" and taking the Lady Nerralina from his coat-tail pocket, he put her carefully upon the table.

Every face in the room was in an instant the picture of horror,—all but of the little girl whose duty it was to fasten Nerralina's dress every morning,— who got behind the door, and jumping up, and clapping her hands and heels, exclaimed, "Good! good! Now she can see to fasten her own frock behind!"

The Prince was the first to move, and, with tears in his eyes, he approached the luckless lady, who was sobbing piteously.

"Poor thing!" said he, and, putting his arm around her, he kissed her. What joy thrilled through Nerralina! She had never been kissed by a man before, and it did for her what such things have done for many a young lady since—it turned her head!

"Blow, horners, blow!" shouted the King. "Join hands all!"

Seizing Nerralina's hand, and followed by the Prince and Princess, who sprang from the table, he

led off the five thousand couples in a grand gallo-
pade.

The Giant stood, and laughed heartily, until, at
last, being no longer able to restrain himself, he
sprang into the midst of them, and danced away royally, trampling about twenty couples under foot at
every jump.

"Dance away, old fellow!" shouted the King, from
the other end of the room. "Dance away, my boy,
and never mind the people."

And the music blew louder, and round they all
went faster and faster, until the building shook and
trembled from the cellar to the roof.

At length, perfectly exhausted, they all stopped,
and Ting-a-ling, slipping down from the Giant's frill,
went out of the door.

"O!" said he, wiping the tears of laughter from
his eyes, "it was all so funny, and every body was
so happy—that—that I almost forgot my bereave-
ment."

Ting-a-ling and
the Five Magicians

TING-A-LING, FOR some weeks after the death of
his young companion, Ling-a-ting, seemed
quite sad and dejected. He spent nearly all
his time lying in a half-opened rose-bud, and thinking of the dear little creature who was gone. But
one morning, the bud having become a full-blown
rose, its petals fell apart, and dropped little Ting-a-
ling out on the grass. The sudden fall did not hurt
him, but it roused him to exertion, and he said, "O
ho! This will never do. I will go up to the palace, and
see if there is anything going on." So off he went
to the great palace; and sure enough something was
going on. He had scarcely reached the court-yard,
when the bells began to ring, the horns to blow, the
drums to beat, and crowds of people to shout and
run in every direction, and there was never such a
noise and hubbub before.

Ting-a-ling slipped along close to the wall, so that

he would not be stepped on by anybody; and having reached the palace, he climbed up a long trailing vine, into one of the lower windows. There he saw the vast audience-chamber filled with people, shouting, and calling, and talking, all at once. The grand vizier was on the wide platform of the throne, making a speech, but the uproar was so great that not one word of it could Ting-a-ling hear. The King himself was by his throne, putting on the bulky boots, which he only wore when he went to battle, and which made him look so terrible that a person could hardly see him without trembling. The last time that he had worn those boots, as Ting-a-ling very well knew, he had made war on a neighboring country, and had defeated all the armies, killed all the people, torn down all the towns and cities, and every house and cottage, and ploughed up the whole country, and sowed it with thistles, so that it could never be used as a country any more. So Ting-a-ling thought that as the King was putting on his war boots, something very great was surely about to happen. Hearing a fizzing noise behind him, he turned around, and there was the Prince in the court-yard, grinding his sword on the grindstone, which was turned by two slaves, who were working away so hard and fast that they were nearly ready to drop. Then he *knew* that wonderful things were surely coming to pass, for in ordinary times the Prince never lifted his finger to do anything for himself.

Just then, a little page, who had been sent for the King's spurs, and couldn't find them, and who was therefore afraid to go back, stopped to rest himself for a minute against the window where Ting-a-ling was standing. As his head just reached a little above the windowseat, Ting-a-ling went close to his ear and shouted to him, to please tell him what was the matter. The page started at first, but, seeing it was only a little fairy, he told him that the Princess was lost, and that the whole army was going out to find her. Before he could say anything more, the King was heard to roar for his spurs, and away ran the little page, whether to look again for the spurs, or to hide himself, is not known at the present day. Ting-a-ling now became very much excited. The Princess Aufalia, who had been married to the Prince but a month ago, was very dear to him, and he felt that he must do something for her. But while he was thinking what this something might possibly be, he heard the clear and distinct sound of a tiny bell, which however, no one but a fairy could possibly have heard above all that noise. He knew it was the bell of the fairy Queen, summoning her subjects to her presence; and in a moment he slid down the vine, and scampered away to the gardens. There, although the sun was shining brightly, and the fairies seldom assembled but by night, there were great crowds of them, all listening to the Queen, and keeping much better order than the people in the King's palace. The Queen addressed them in soul-stirring strains, and urged every one to do their best to find the missing Princess. In the night she had been taken away, while the Prince and everybody were asleep. "And now," said the Queen, untying her scarf, and holding it up, "away with you, every one! Search every house, garden, mountain, and plain, in the land, and the first one who comes to me with news of the Princess Aufalia, shall wear my scarf!" And, as this was a mark of high distinction, and conveyed privileges of which there is no time now to tell, the fairies gave a great cheer (which would have sounded to you, had you heard it, like a puff of wind through a thicket of reeds), and they all rushed away in every direction. Now, though the fairies of this tribe could go almost anywhere, through small cracks and key-holes, under doors, and into places where no one else could possibly penetrate, they did not fly, or float in the air, or anything of that sort. When they wished to travel fast or far, they would mount on butterflies, and all sorts of insects; but they seldom needed such assistance, as they were not in the habit of going far from their homes in the palace gardens. Ting-a-ling ran, as fast as he could, to where a friend of his, whom we have mentioned before, kept grasshoppers and butterflies to hire; but he found he was too late,—every one of them was taken by the fairies who had got there before him.

"Never mind," said Ting-a-ling to himself, "I'll catch a wild one"; and, borrowing a bridle, he went out into the meadows, to catch a grasshopper for himself. He soon perceived one, quietly feeding under a clover-blossom. Ting-a-ling slipped up softly behind him; but the grasshopper heard him, and rolled his big eyes backward, drawing in his hind-legs in the way which all boys know so well. "What's the good of his seeing all around him?" thought Ting-a-ling; but there is no doubt that the grasshopper thought there was a great deal of good in it, for, just as Ting-a-ling made a rush at him, he let fly with one of his hind-legs, and kicked our little friend so high into the air, that he thought he was never coming down again. He landed, however, harmlessly on the grass on the other side of a fence. Nothing discouraged, he jumped up, with his bridle still in his hand, and looked around for the grasshopper. There he was, with his eyes still rolled back, and his leg ready for another kick, should Ting-a-ling approach him again. But the little fellow had had enough of those strong legs, and so he slipped along the fence, and, getting through it, stole around in front of the grasshopper; and, while he was still looking backward with all his eyes, Ting-a-ling stepped quietly up before him, and slipped the bridle over his head! It was of no use for the grasshopper to struggle and pull back, for Ting-a-ling was astraddle of him in a moment, kicking him with his heels, and shouting "Hi! Hi!"

Away sprang the grasshopper like a bird, and he sped on and on, faster than he had ever gone before in his life, and Ting-a-ling waved his little sword over his head, and shouted "Hi! Hi!"

So on they went for a long time; and in the afternoon the grasshopper began to get very tired, and did not make anything like such long jumps as he had done at first. They were going down a grassy hill, and had just reached the bottom, when Ting-a-ling heard some one calling him. Looking around him in astonishment, he saw that it was a little fairy of his acquaintance, younger than himself, named Parsley, who was sitting in the shade of a wide-spreading dandelion.

"Hello, Parsley!" cried Ting-a-ling, reining up. "What are you doing there?"

"Why you see, Ting-a-ling," said the other, "I came out to look for the Princess"—

"You!" cried Ting-a-ling; "a little fellow like you!"

"Yes, *I*!" cried Parsley; "and Sourgrass and I rode the same butterfly; but by the time we had come this far, we got too heavy, and Sourgrass made me get off."

"And what are you going to do now?" said Ting-a-ling.

"O, I'm all right!" replied Parsley. "I shall have a butterfly of my own soon."

"How's that?" asked Ting-a-ling, quite curious to know.

"Come here!" said Parsley; and so Ting-a-ling got off his grasshopper, and led it up close to his friend. "See what I've found!" said Parsley, showing a cocoon that lay beside him. "I'm going to wait till this butterfly's hatched, and I shall have him the minute he comes out."

The idea of waiting for the butterfly to be hatched, seemed so funny to Ting-a-ling, that he burst out laughing, and Parsley laughed too, and so did the grasshopper, for he took this opportunity to slip his head out of the bridle, and away he went!

Ting-a-ling turned and gazed in amazement at the grasshopper skipping up the hill; and Parsley, when he had done laughing, advised him to hunt around for another cocoon, and follow his example.

Ting-a-ling did not reply to this advice, but throwing his bridle to Parsley, said, "There, you would better take that. You may want it when your butterfly's hatched. I shall push on."

"What! Walk?" cried Parsley.

"Yes, walk," said Ting-a-ling. "Good-by."

So Ting-a-ling travelled on by himself for the rest of the day, and it was nearly evening when he came to a wide brook with beautiful green banks, and overhanging trees. Here he sat down to rest himself; and while he was wondering if it would be a good thing for him to try to get across, he amused himself by watching the sports and antics of various insects and fishes that were enjoying themselves that fine summer evening. Plenty of butterflies and dragonflies were there, but Ting-a-ling knew that he could never catch one of them, for they were nearly all the time over the surface of the water; and many a big fish was watching them from below, hoping that in their giddy flights, some of them would come near enough to be snapped down for supper. There were spiders, who shot over the surface of the brook as if they had been skating; and all sorts of beautiful bugs and flies were there,—green, yellow, emerald, gold, and black. At a short distance, Ting-a-ling saw a crowd of little minnows, who had caught a young tadpole, and, having tied a bluebell to his tail, were now chasing the affrighted creature about. But after a while the tadpole's mother came out, and then the minnows caught it!

While watching all these lively creatures, Ting-a-ling fell asleep, and when he awoke, it was dark night. He jumped up, and looked about him. The butterflies and dragon-flies had all gone to bed, and now the great night-bugs and buzzing beetles were out; the katydids were chirping in the trees, and the frogs were croaking among the long reeds. Not far off, on the same side of the brook, Ting-a-ling saw the light of a fire, and so he walked over to see what it meant. On his way, he came across some wild honeysuckles, and, pulling one of the blossoms, he sucked out the sweet juice for his supper, as he walked along. When he reached the fire, he saw sitting around it five men, with turbans and great black beards. Ting-a-ling instantly perceived that they were magicians, and, putting the honeysuckle to his lips, he blew a little tune upon it, which the magicians hearing, they said to one another, "There is a fairy near us." Then Ting-a-ling came into the midst of them, and, climbing up on a pile of cloaks and shawls, conversed with them; and he soon heard that they knew, by means of their magical arts, that the Princess had been stolen the night before, by the slaves of a wicked dwarf, and that she was now locked up in his castle, which was on top of a high mountain, and far from where they then were.

"I shall go there right off," said Ting-a-ling.

"And what will you do when you get there?" said the youngest magician, whose name was Zamcar. "This dwarf is a terrible little fellow, and the same one who twisted poor Nerralina's head, which circumstance of course you remember. He has numbers of fierce slaves, and a great castle. You are a good little fellow, but I don't think you could do much for the Princess, if you did go to her."

Ting-a-ling reflected a moment, and then said that he would go to his friend, the Giant Tur-il-i-ra; but Zamcar told him that that tremendous individual had gone to the uttermost limits of China, to launch a ship. It was such a big one, and so heavy, that it had sunk down into the earth as tight as if it had grown there, and all the men and horses in the country could not move it. So there was nothing to do but to send for Tur-il-i-ra. When Ting-a-ling heard this, he was disheartened, and hung his little head. "The best thing to do," remarked Alcahazar, the oldest of the magicians, "would be to inform the King and his army of the place where the Princess is confined, and let them go and take her out."

"O no!" cried Ting-a-ling, who, if his body was no larger than a very small pea-pod, had a soul as big as a water-melon. "If the King knows it, up he will come with all his drums and horns, and the dwarf will hear him a mile off, and either kill the Princess, or hide her away. If we were all to go to the castle, I should think we could do something ourselves." This was the longest speech that Ting-a-ling had ever made; and when he was through, the youngest magician said to the others that he thought it was growing cooler, and the others agreed that it was. After some conversation among themselves in an exceedingly foreign tongue, these kind magicians agreed to go up to the castle, and see what they could do. So Zamcar put Ting-a-ling in the folds of his turban, and the whole party started off for the dwarf's castle. They looked like a company of travelling merchants, each one having a package on his back and a great staff in his hand. When they reached the outer gate of the castle, Alcahazar, the oldest, knocked at it with his stick, and it was opened at once by a shiny black slave, who, coming out, shut it behind him, and inquired what the travellers wanted.

"Is your master within?" asked Alcahazar.

"I don't know," said the slave.

"Can you find out?" asked the magician.

"Well, good merchant, perhaps I might; but I don't particularly want to know," said the slave, as he leaned back against the gate, leisurely striking with his long sword at the night-bugs and beetles that were buzzing about.

"My friend," said Alcahazar, "don't you think that is rather a careless way of using a sword? You might cut somebody."

"That's true," said the slave. "I didn't think of it before"; but he kept on striking away, all the same.

"Then stop it!" said Alcahazar, the oldest magician, striking the sword from his hand with one blow of his staff. Upon this, up stepped Ormanduz, the next oldest, and whacked the slave over his head; and then Mahalla, the next oldest, struck him over the shoulders; and Akbeck, the next oldest, cracked him on the shins; and Zamcar, the youngest, punched him in the stomach; and the slave sat down, and begged the noble merchants to please stop. So they stopped, and he humbly informed them that his master was in.

"We would see him," said Alcahazar.

"But, sirs," said the slave, "he is having a grand feast."

"Well," said the magician, "we're invited."

"O noble merchants!" cried the slave, "why did you not tell me that before?" and he opened wide the gate, and let them in. After they had passed the outer gate, which was of wood, they went through another of iron, and another of brass, and another of copper, and then walked through the court-yard, filled with armed slaves, and up the great castle steps; at the top of which stood the butler, dressed in gorgeous array.

"Whom have you here, base slave?" cried the gorgeous butler.

"Five noble merchants, invited to my lord's feast," said the slave, bowing to the ground.

"But they cannot enter the banqueting hall in such garbs," said the butler. "They cannot be noble merchants, if they come not nobly dressed to my lord's feast."

"O sir!" said Alcahazar, "may your delicate and far-reaching understanding be written in books, and taught to youth in foreign lands, and may your profound judgment ever overawe your country! But allow us now to tell you that we have gorgeous dresses in these our packs. Would we soil them with the dust of travel, ere we entered the halls of my lord the dwarf?"

The butler bowed low at this address, and caused the five magicians to be conducted to five magnificent chambers, where were slaves, and lights, and baths, and soap, and towels, and wash-rags, and tooth-brushes; and each magician took a gorgeous dress from his pack, and put it on, and then they were all conducted (with Ting-a-ling still in Zamcar's turban) to the grand hall, where the feast was being held. Here they found the dwarf and his guests, numbering a hundred, having a truly jolly time. The dwarf, who was dressed in white (to make him look larger), was seated on a high red velvet cushion at the end of the hall, and the company sat cross-legged on rugs, in a great circle before him. He was drinking out of a huge bottle nearly as big as himself, and eating little birds; and judging by the bones that were left, he must have eaten nearly a whole flock of them. When he saw the five magicians entering, he stopped eating, and opened his eyes in amazement, and then shouted to his servants to tell him who these people were, who came without permission to his feast; but as no one knew, nobody answered. The guests, seeing the stately demeanor and magnificent dresses of the visitors, thought that they were at least five great monarchs.

"My lord the dwarf," said Alcahazar, advancing toward him, "I am the king of a far country; and passing your castle, and hearing of your feast, I have made bold to come and offer you some of the sweet-tasting birds of my kingdom." So saying, he lifted up his richly embroidered cloak, and took from under it a great silver dish containing about two hundred dozen hot, smoking, delicately cooked, fat little birds. Under the dish were fastened lamps of perfumed oil, all lighted, and keeping the savory food nice and hot. Making a low bow, the magician placed the dish before the dwarf, who tasted one of the birds, and immediately clapped his hands with joy. "Great King!" he cried, "welcome to my feast! Slaves, quick! make room for the great king!" As there was no vacant place, the slaves took hold of one of the guests, and gave him what the boys would call a "hist," right through the window, and Alcahazar took his place. Then stepped forward Ormanduz, and said, "My lord the dwarf, I am also the king of a far country, and I have made bold to offer you some of the wine of my kingdom." So saying, he lifted his gold-lined cloak, and took from beneath it a crystal decanter, covered with gold and ruby ornaments, with one hundred and one beautifully carved silver goblets hanging from its neck, and which contained about eleven gallons of the most delicious wine. He placed it before the dwarf, who, having tasted the wine, gave a great cheer, and shouted to his slaves to make room for this mighty king. So the slaves took another guest by the neck and heels, and sent him, slam-bang, through the window, and Ormanduz took his place. Then stepped forward Mahallah, and said, "My lord the dwarf, I am also the king of a far country, and I bring you a sample of the venison of my kingdom." So saying, he raised his velvet cloak, trimmed with diamonds, and took from under it a whole deer, already cooked, and stuffed with oysters, anchovies, buttered toast, olives, tamarind seeds, sweetmarjoram, sage, and many other herbs and spices, and all piping hot, and smelling deliciously. This he put down before the dwarf, who, when he had tasted it, waved his goblet over his head, and cried out to the slaves to make room for this mighty king. So the slaves seized another guest and out of the window, like a shot, he went, and Mahallah took his place. Then Akbeck stepped up, and said, "My lord the dwarf, I am also the king of a far country, and I bring you some of the confections of my dominions." So saying, he took from under his cloak of gold cloth, a great basket of silver filagree work, in which were cream-chocolates, and burnt almonds, and sponge-cake, and lady's fingers, and mixtures, and gingernuts, and hoar hound candy, and gumdrops, and fruit-cake, and cream candy, and mint-stick, and pound-cake, and rock candy, and butter taffy, and many other confections, amounting in all to about two hundred and twenty pounds. He placed the basket before the dwarf, who tasted some of these good things, and found them so delicious, that he lay on his back and kicked up his heels in delight, shouting to his slaves to make room for this great king. As the next guest was a big, fat man, too heavy to throw far, he was seized by four slaves, who walked him Spanish right out of the door, and Akbeck took his place. Then Zamcar stepped forward and said, "My lord the dwarf, I also am king of a far country, and I bring you some of the fruit of my dominions." And so saying, he took from beneath his gold and purple cloak, a great basket filled with currants as big as grapes, and grapes as big as plums, and plums as big as peaches, and peaches as big cantaloupes, and cantaloupes as big as watermelons, and water-melons as big as barrels. There were about nineteen bushels of them altogether, and he put them before the dwarf, who, having tasted some of them, clapped his hands, and shouted to his slaves to make room for this mighty king; but as the next guest had very sensibly got up and gone out, Zamcar took his seat without any delay. Then Ting-a-ling, who was very much excited by all these wonderful performances, slipped down out of Zamcar's turban, and, running up towards the dwarf, cried out, "My lord the dwarf, I am also the king of a far country, and I bring you"—and he lifted up his little cloak; but as there was nothing there, he said no more, but clambered up into Zamcar's turban again. As nobody noticed or heard him, so great was the bustle and noise of the festivity, his speech made no difference one way or the other. After everybody had eaten and drunk until they could eat and drink no more, the dwarf jumped up and called to the chief butler, to know how many beds were prepared for the guests; to which the butler answered that there were thirty beds prepared. "Then," said the dwarf, "give these five noble kings each one of the best rooms, with a down bed, and a silken comfortable; and give the other beds to the twenty-five biggest guests. As to the rest, turn them out!" So the dwarf went to bed, and each of the magicians had a splendid room, and twenty-five of the biggest guests had beds, and the rest were all turned out. As it was pouring down rain, and freezing, and cold, and wet, and slippery (for the weather was very unsettled on this mountain), and all these guests, who now found themselves outside of the castle gates, lived many miles away, and as none of them had any hats, or knew the way home, they were very miserable indeed.

Alcahazar did not go to bed, but sat in his room and reflected. He saw that the dwarf had given this feast on account of his joy at having captured the Princess, and thus caused grief to the King and Prince, and all the people; but it was also evident that he was very sly, and had not mentioned the matter to any of the company. The other magicians did not go to bed either, but sat in their rooms, and thought the same thing; and Ting-a-ling, in Zamcar's turban, was of exactly the same opinion. So, in about an hour, when all was still, the magicians got up, and went softly over the castle. One went down into the lower rooms, and there were all the slaves, fast asleep; and another into one wing of the castle, and there were half the guests, fast asleep; and another into the other wing, and there were the rest of the guests, fast asleep; and Alcahazar went into the dwarf's room, in the centre of the castle, and there was he, fast asleep, with one of his fists shut tight. The magician touched his fist with his magic staff, and it immediately opened, and there was a key! So Alcahazar took the key, and shut up the dwarf's hand again. Zamcar went up to the floor, near the top of the house, and entered a large room, which was empty, but the walls were hung with curtains made of snakes' skins, beautifully woven together. Ting-a-ling slipped down to the floor, and, peeping behind these curtains, saw the hinge of a door; and without saying a word, he got behind the curtain, and, sure enough, there was a door! and there was a key-hole! and in a minute, there was Ting-a-ling right through it! and there was the Princess in a chair in the middle of a great room, crying as if her heart would break! By the light of the moon, which had now broken through the clouds, Ting-a-ling saw that she was tied fast to the chair. So he climbed up on her shoulder, and called her by name; and when the Princess heard him and knew him, she took him into her lovely hands, and kissed him, and cried over him, and laughed over him so much, that her joy had like to have been the death of him. When she got over her excitement, she told him how she had been stolen away; how she had heard her favorite cat squeak in the middle of the night, and how she had got up quickly to go to it, supposing it had been squeezed in some door, and how the wicked dwarf, who had been imitating the cat, was just outside the door with his slaves; and how they had seized her, and bound her, and carried her off to this castle, without waking up any of the King's household. Then Ting-a-ling told her that his five friends were there, and that they were going to see what they could do; and the Princess was very glad to hear that, you may be sure. Then Ting-a-ling slipped down to the floor, and through the key-hole; and as he entered the room where he had left Zamcar, in came Alcahazar with the key, and the other magicians with news that everybody was asleep. When Ting-a-ling had told about the Princess, Alcahazar pushed aside the curtains, unlocked the door with the key, and they all entered the next room.

There, sure enough, was the Princess Aufalia; but, right in front of her, on the floor, squatted the dwarf, who had missed his key, and had slipped up by a back way! The magicians started back on seeing him; the Princess was crying bitterly, and Ting-a-ling ran past the dwarf (who was laughing too horribly to notice him), and climbing upon the Princess's shoulder, sat there among her curls, and did his best to comfort her.

"Anyway," said he, "*I* shall not leave you again," and he drew his little sword, and felt as big as a house. The magicians now advanced towards the dwarf; but he, it seems, was a bit of a magician himself, for he waved a little wand, and instantly a strong partition of iron wire rose up out of the floor, and, reaching from one wall to the other, separated him completely from the five men. The magicians no sooner saw this, than they cried out, "O ho! Mr. Dwarf, is that your game?"

"Yes," said the little wretch, chuckling; "can you play at it?"

"A little," said they; and each one pulled from under his cloak a long file; and filing the partition from the wall on each side, which only needed a few strokes from their sharp files, they pulled it entirely down. But before the magicians could reach him, the dwarf again waved his wand, and a great chasm opened in the floor before them, which was too wide to jump over, and so deep that the bottom could not be seen.

"O ho!" cried the magicians; "another game, eh!"

"Yes indeed," cried the dwarf. "Just let me see you play at *that*."

Each of the magicians then took from under his magic cloak a long board, and, putting them over the chasm, they began to walk across them. But the dwarf jumped up and waved his wand, and water commenced to fall on the boards, where it immediately froze; and they were so slippery, that the magicians could hardly keep their feet, and could not make one step forward. Even standing still, they came very near falling off into the chasm below. "I suppose you can play at that," said the dwarf; and the magicians replied: "O yes!" and each one took from under his cloak a pan of ashes, and sprinkled the boards, and walked right over. But before they reached the other edge, the dwarf pushed the chair, which was on rollers, up against the wall behind him, which opened; and instantly the Princess, Ting-a-ling, and the dwarf disappeared, and the wall closed up. Without saying a word, the magicians each drew from beneath his cloak a pickaxe, and they cut a hole in the wall in a few minutes. There was a large room on the other side, but it was entirely empty. So they sat down, and got out their magical calculators, and soon discovered that the Princess was in the lowest part of the castle; but the magical calculators being a little out of order, they could not show exactly her place of confinement. Then the five hurried down-stairs, where they found the slaves still asleep; but one poor little boy, whose business it was to get up early every morning and split kindling wood, having had none of the feast, was not very sleepy, and woke up when he heard footsteps near him. The magicians asked him if he could show them to the lowest part of the castle. "All right," said he; "this way"; and he led them to where there was a great black hole, with a windlass over it. "Get in the bucket," said he, "and I will lower you down."

"Bucket!" cried Alcahazar. "Is that a well?"

"To be sure it is," said the boy, who had nothing on but the baby-clothes he had worn ever since he was born; and which, as he was now about ten years old, had split a good deal in the back and arms, but in length they were very suitable.

"But there can be no one down there," said the magician. "I see deep water."

"Of course there is nobody there," replied the boy. "Were you told to go down there to meet anybody? Because, if you were, you had better take some tubs down with you, to sit in. But all I know about it is, that it's the lowest part of this old hole of a castle."

"Boy," said Alcahazar, "there is a young lady shut up down here somewhere. Do you know where she is?"

"How old is she?" asked the boy.

"About seventeen," said the magician.

"O then! if she is no older than that, I should think she'd be in the preserve-closet, if she knew where it was," and the boy pointed to a great door, barred and locked, where the dwarf, who had a very sweet tooth, kept all his preserves locked up tight and fast. Zamcar stooped and looked through the key-hole of this door, and there, sure enough, was the Princess! So the boy proved to be smarter than all the magicians. Each of our five friends now took from under his cloak a crowbar, and in a minute they had forced open the great door. But they had scarcely entered, when the dwarf, springing on the arm of the chair to which the Princess was still tied, drew his sword, and clapped it to her throat, crying out, that if the magicians came one step nearer, he would slice her head off.

"O ho!" cried they, "is that your game?"

"Yes indeed," said the chuckling dwarf; "can you play at it?"

The magicians did not appear to think that they could; but Ting-a-ling, who was still on the Princess's shoulder, though unseen by the dwarf, suddenly shouted, "I can play!" and in an instant he had driven his little sword into the dwarf's eye, who immediately sprang from the chair with a howl of anguish. While he was yelling and skipping about, with his hands to his eyes, the poor boy, who hated him worse than pills, clapped a great jar of preserves over him, and sat down on the bottom of the jar! The magicians then untied the Princess; and as she looked weak and faint, Zamcar, the youngest, took from under his cloak a little table, set with everything hot and nice for supper; and when the Princess had eaten something and taken a cup of tea, she felt a great deal better. Alcahazar lifted up the jar from the dwarf, and there was the little rascal, so covered up with sticky jam, that he could not speak and could hardly move. So, taking an oil-cloth bag from under his cloak, Alcahazar dropped the dwarf into it, and tied it up, and hung it to his girdle. The two youngest magicians made a sort of chair out of a shawl, and they carried the Princess on it between them, very comfortably; and as Ting-a-ling still remained on her shoulder, she began to feel that things were beginning to look brighter.

They then asked the poor boy what he would like best as a reward for what he had done; and he said that if they would shut him up in that room, and lock the door tight, and lose the key, he would be happy all the days of his life. So they left the boy (who knew what was good, and was already sucking away at a jar of preserved greengages) in the room, and they shut the door and locked it tight, and lost the key; and he lived there for ninety-one years, eating preserves; and when they were all gone, he died. All that time he never had any clothes but his baby-clothes, and they got pretty sticky before his death. Then our party left the castle; and as they passed the slaves still fast asleep, the three oldest magicians took from under their cloaks watering-pots, filled with water that makes men sleep, and they watered the slaves with it, until they were wet enough to sleep a week. When they went through the gates of copper, brass, iron, and wood, they left them all open behind them. They had not gone far before they saw seventy-five men, all sitting in a row at the side of the road, and looking woefully indeed. They had been wet to the skin, and were now frozen stiff, not one of them being able to move anything but his eyelids, and they were all crying as if their hearts would break. So the magicians stopped, and the three oldest each took from under his cloak a pair of bellows, and they blew hot air on the poor creatures until they were all thawed. Then Alcahazar told them to go up to the castle, and take it for their own, and live there all the rest of their lives. He informed them that the dwarf was his prisoner, and that the slaves would sleep for a week.

When the seventy-five guests (for those who had been taken from the feast, had joined their comrades) heard this, they all started up, and ran like deer for the castle; and when they reached it, they woke up their comrades, and took possession, and lived there all their lives. The man who had been first thrown through the window, and who had broken the way through the glass for the others, was elected their chief, because he had suffered the most; and excepting the trouble of doing their own work for a week, until the slaves awoke, these people were very happy ever afterwards.

It was just daylight when our party left the dwarf's castle, and by the next evening they had reached the palace. The army had not got back, and there was no one there but the ladies of the Princess. When these saw their dear mistress, there was never before such a kissing, and hugging, and crying, and laughing. Ting-a-ling came in for a good share of praise and caressing; and if he had not slipped away to tell his tale to the fairy Queen, there is no knowing what would have become of him. The magicians sat down outside of the Princess's apartments, to guard her until the army should return; and the ladies would have kissed and hugged them, in their gratitude and joy, if they had not been such dignified and grave personages.

Now, the King, the Prince, and the great army, had gone miles and miles away in the opposite direction to the dwarf's castle, and the Princess and her ladies could not think how to let them know what had happened. As for ringing the great bell, they knew that that would be useless, for they would never hear it at the distance they were, and so they wished that they had some fireworks to set off. Therefore Zamcar, the youngest magician, offered to go up to the top of the palace and set off some. So, when he got up to the roof, he lifted up his cloak, and took out some fireworks, and set them off; and the light shone for miles and miles, and the King and all his army saw it. The King had just begun to feel tired, and to think that he would pitch his tent, and rest for the night by the side of a pleasant stream they had reached, when he saw the light from the palace, and instantly knew that there had been tidings of the Princess,—kings are so smart, you know. So, when his slaves came to ask him where they should pitch his tent, he shouted, "Pitch it in the river! 'Tention, army! Right about face, for home,—MARCH!" and away the whole army marched for home, the band playing the lively air of

"Cream cakes for supper,
Heigh O! Heigh O!
O! Cream cakes for supper
Heigh O! Heigh O!"—

so as to keep up the spirits of the tired men. When they approached the palace, which was all lighted up, there was the Princess standing at the great door, in her Sunday clothes, and looking as lovely as a full-blown rose. The King jumped from his high-mettled racer, and went up the steps, two at a time; but the Prince, springing from his fiery steed, bounded up three steps at once, and got there first. When he and the King had got through hugging and kissing the Princess, her Sunday clothes looked as if they had been worn a week.

"Now then for supper," said the King, "and I hope it's ready." But the Princess said never a word, for she had forgotten all about supper; and all the ladies hung their heads, and were afraid to speak. But when they reached the great hall, they found that the magicians had been at work, and had cooked a grand supper. There it was, on ever so many long tables, all smoking hot, and smelling delightfully. So they all sat down, for there was room enough for every man, and nobody said a word until he was as tight as a drum.

When they had all had enough, and were just about to begin to talk, there were heard strains of the most delightful soft music; and directly, in at a window came the Queen of fairies, attended by her court, all mounted on beautiful golden moths and dragon-flies. When they reached the velvet table in front of the throne, where the King had been eating, with his plate on his lap, they arranged themselves in a circle on the table, and the Queen spoke out in a clear little voice, that could have been heard almost anywhere, and announced to the King that the little Ting-a-ling, who now wore her royal scarf, was the preserver of his daughter.

"O ho!" said the King; "and what can I do for such a mite as you, my fine little fellow?"

Then Ting-a-ling, who wanted nothing for himself, and only thought of the good of his people, made a low bow to the King, and shouted at the top of his voice, "Your royal gardeners are going to make asparagus beds all over our fairy pleasure grounds. If you can prevent that, I have nothing more to ask."

"Blow, Horner, blow!" cried the King, "and hear, all men! If any man, woman, or child, from this time henceforward forever, shall dare to set foot in the garden now occupied by the fairies, he shall be put to death, he and all his family, and his relations, as far as they can be traced. Take notice of that, every one of you!"

Ting-a-ling then bowed his thanks, and all the people made up their minds to take very particular notice of what the King had said.

Then the magicians were ordered to come forward and name their reward; but they bowed their heads, and simply besought the King that he would grant them seven rye straws, the peeling from a red apple, and the heel from one of his old slippers. What in the name of common sense they wanted with these, no one but themselves knew; but magicians are such strange creatures! When these valuable gifts had been bestowed upon them, the five good magicians departed, leaving the dwarf for the King to do what he pleased with. This little wretch was shut up in an iron cage, and every day was obliged to eat three codfish, a bushel of Irish potatoes, and eleven pounds of bran crackers, and to drink a gallon of cambric tea; all of which things he despised from the bottom of his miserable little heart.

"Now," cried the King, "all is settled, and let everybody to go to bed. There is room enough in the palace for all to sleep to-night. Form in line, and to bed,—MARCH!" So they all formed in line, and began to march to bed, to the music of the band; and the fairies, their little horns blowing, and with Ting-a-ling at the post of honor by the Queen, took up their line of march, out of the window to the garden, which was to be, henceforward forever, their own. Just as they were all filing out, in flew little Parsley on the back of his butterfly, which had been hatched out at last.

"Hello!" cried he. "Is it all over?"

"Pretty nearly," said Ting-a-ling. "It's just letting out. How came you to be so late?"

"Easy enough," said poor little Parsley. "Of all the mean things that ever was the pokiest long time in unwrapping its wings, this butterfly's the meanest."

192

Ting-a-ling's Visit to Tur-il-i-ra

ONE PLEASANT sunny day, the Giant Tur-il-i-ra was lying on his back on the grass, under some great trees, in a wood near the palace of the King.

His feet were high above the rest of his body, resting in the crotch of a great oak-tree, and he lay with his vest open and his hat off, idly sucking the pith from a young sapsago-tree that he had just broken off. Near him, on the top of a tall bulrush, sat the little fairy Ting-a-ling. They had been talking together for some time, and Tur-il-i-ra said, "Ting-a-ling, you must come and see me. You have never been to my castle except when you came for the good of somebody else. Come now for yours and mine, and stay at least a week. We will have a gay old time. Will you come?"

"I will," cried the little fairy, in a voice as clear

as the chirp of a cricket. "I'll come whenever you say so."

"Let it be to-morrow, then," said the Giant. "Shall I fetch you?"

"O no," said Ting-a-ling; "I will come on my blue butterfly. You have no idea how fast he flies. I do believe he could go to your castle nearly as fast as you could yourself."

"All right," said Tur-il-i-ra, rising. "Come as you please, but be sure you come to stay."

Then the Giant got up, and he shook himself, and buttoned his vest, and put on his hat, and as he had thin boots on, he told Ting-a-ling he was going to see if he couldn't take the river at one jump. So, tightening his belt, and going back for a good run, he rushed to the river bank, and with a spring like the jerk of five mad elephants, he bounded across. But the opposite bank was not hard enough to resist the tremendous fall of so many tons of giant as came upon it when Tur-il-i-ra's feet touched its edge; and it gave way, and his feet went up and his back came down, and into the river, like a ship dropping out of the sky, went the mighty Giant. The splash was so great that the whole air, for a minute or two, was full of water and spray, and Ting-a-ling could see nothing at all. When things had become visible again, there was Tur-il-i-ra standing up to the middle of his thighs in the channel of the river, and brushing from his eyes and his nose the water that trickled from him like little brooks.

"Hel-l-o-o-o!" cried Ting-a-ling. "Are you hurt?"

"O no!" sputtered the Giant. "The water and the mud were soft enough, but I'm nearly blinded and choked."

"It's a good thing it isn't worse," cried the fairy.

"If that river had not been so broad, you would have broken your neck when you came down."

"Good-by!" cried the Giant, stepping upon the bank, "I must hurry home as fast as I can." And so away he went over the hills at a run, and you may rest assured that he did not jump any more rivers that day.

The next morning early, Ting-a-ling mounted his blue butterfly, and over the field he went almost as fast as a bird, for his was a butterfly of the desert, where they have to fly very far for anything to eat, and to race for it very often at that. Ting-a-ling took nothing with him but what he wore, but his "things" and his best clothes were to be sent after him on a beetle, which, though slow, was very strong, and could have carried, if he chose, everything that Ting-a-ling had. About sunset, the fairy and the butterfly, the latter very tired, arrived at the castle of Tur-il-i-ra, and there, at the great door, stood the Giant, expecting them, with his face beaming with hospitality and delight. He had had his slaves, for the whole afternoon, scattered along the road by which his visitor would come; and they were commanded to keep a sharp lookout for a blue butterfly, and pass the word to the castle when they saw it coming. So Tur-il-i-ra was all ready; and as he held out his finger, the butterfly was glad enough to fly up and light upon it. The good Giant took them both into the house, and the butterfly was put on a top-shelf, where there were some honey-jars, and if he didn't eat!

Supper was all ready, and Tur-il-i-ra sat down to the table on a chair which was bigger than some houses, while Ting-a-ling sat cross-legged on a napkin, opposite to him. The Giant had everything nice. There was a pair of roast oxen, besides a small boiled whale, and a great plate of fricasseed elks. As for vegetables, there were boat-loads of mashed potatoes, and turnips, and beans; and there was a pie which was as big as a small back-yard. The Giant had a splendid appetite, and before supper was over he had eaten up most of these things. As for little Ting-a-ling, he had only got half way through his third grain of boiled rice, when the Giant was done. But he could eat no more; and after scooping up about a drop of wine in a little cup he carried with him, he drank the health of Tur-il-i-ra, and then they went out on the front porch, where the Giant ordered his big pipe to be brought, and he had a smoke. When Tur-il-i-ra had finished his pipe, and Ting-a-ling had nearly sneezed himself to death, and the whole atmosphere, for about a mile around the castle, was foggy with smoke, they went in to bed.

Tur-il-i-ra took Ting-a-ling up-stairs, and showed him where he was to sleep; and then putting him down on the bed, he bade him good-night, and went out and shut the door after him.

Ting-a-ling stood in the middle of the bed and looked about him. It was as if he was in the midst of a great plain. The bed was a double one, that had belonged to the Giant's father and mother, and he had given it to Ting-a-ling because it was the best in the house. The little fairy was delighted with this bed, which was very smooth, and covered with a great white counterpane. He ran from one end to the other of it, and he turned heels-over-head, and walked on his hands, and amused himself in this way until he was thoroughly tired. Then he lay right down in the very middle, and went to sleep. I would like to have a picture of Ting-a-ling in the Giant's bed, but any one can draw it so easily for himself, that it is of no use to have it here. All that is necessary is to take a large sheet of white paper,—the largest you can get,—and in the centre of it make a small dot,—the smallest you can make,—and there you have the picture.

It must have been nearly morning when Ting-a-ling was awakened by a tremendous knocking at the front-door of the castle. The first thought he had was that perhaps there were his things! But he forgot that a very small, and probably tired-out fairy (for Parsley's younger brother was to come with the baggage), in charge of a beetle in the same condition, could hardly make such a thundering noise as that. But he jumped up and slid down on the floor, and as his room was a front one, he went to the window, and climbing up the curtains, got outside and looked down. There, in the moonlight, he saw an ordinary sized man on horseback, directing about a dozen black slaves, who had hold of a long rope, which they had tied to the knocker of Tur-il-i-ra's door. They were all pulling away at it as hard as they could (and a mighty pounding they made too), when the Giant put his head out of his window, and asked what all this noise meant.

"O good Tur-il-i-ra!" cried the man on the horse, "I have ridden for several days" (he said nothing about his slaves having run all the way) "to come to you, and tell you that the Kyrofatalapynx is loose."

"What!" cried Tur-il-i-ra, in a voice like the explosion of a powder magazine. "Loose!"

"Yes," said the man. "He's been loose for four days."

The Giant pulled in his head, and Ting-a-ling could hear him hurrying down-stairs to open the great door. The man came in and all the slaves, and as a good many of Tur-il-i-ra's people were up by this time, there was a great hubbub of voices in the lower hall; but though Ting-a-ling listened up by the banisters until the cold wind on the staircase had nearly frozen his little bare legs (which were not much longer than your finger-nail, and about as thick as a big darning-needle), he could make out nothing at all of the talk. So he went back to the bed, and got in under the edge of the counterpane, and lay there, with just his head sticking out, until he dropped asleep. At daybreak Tur-il-i-ra came into the room, and stooping over the bed, called to him to get up, as there was to be an early breakfast. As the Giant carried him down-stairs on his finger, he told the fairy that he was deeply grieved, but that he would be obliged to leave him for the rest of the day, on account of the Kyrofatalapynx having broken loose.

"But what is that?" asked Ting-a-ling.

"Why, don't you know? It is a—Look here, you fellows! Didn't I tell you that breakfast was to be all ready when I came down? What do you mean, you lazy rascals? Skip, now, and have everything ready this minute."

And the men skipped, and the cooks cooked, and the fires blazed, and the pots boiled and bubbled, and the Giant sat down in a great hurry, with the man who came on horseback sitting cross-legged on one side of the table, and Ting-a-ling on the other. So he forgot to finish his sentence about the Kyrofatalapynx. During the meal there was nothing but noise and confusion, and Ting-a-ling could not get in a word. The Giant had a dish of broiled sheep before him, and he was crunching them up as fast as he could, and talking, with his mouth full, to the man all the time; and the slaves and the servants were all eating and drinking, and running about, until there was no hearing one's own voice, unless it was a very big one. So, although Ting-a-ling was dying of curiosity to know what the Kyrofatalapynx was, he could not get an answer from any one.

As soon as the Giant was done eating, he jumped up, and shouted for his hat and his boots; and if the men did not run fast enough, he shouted at them all the louder. If Ting-a-ling had not stayed on the table, I don't know what would have become of him in the confusion. The Giant had now pushed off his slippers, and was waiting until the men should bring his boots; and as one lazy fellow was poking round, as if he was half asleep, Tur-il-i-ra was so irritated at his slowness that he slipped the toe of his stockinged foot under him, and gave him a tremendous send right out of the door, and he went flying over the trees at the bottom of the lawn, and over the barley-field on the other side of the ditch, and over the pasture, where the cows were kept, and over the pomegranate orchard, and over the palm-grove by the little lake, and over Hassan ab Kolyar's cottage, right smack down into the soft marsh, back of the sunflower garden; and he didn't get back to the castle until his master had been gone an hour. As the Giant sat on the edge of the table, pulling on his boots, he told Ting-a-ling that he must make himself as comfortable as possible until he came back, and that he would not be gone longer than he could possibly help. But although the fairy asked him again and again to tell him what the Kyrofatalapynx was, he never seemed to hear him, so busy was he, talking to everybody at once. Now Tur-il-i-ra was nearly ready to go, and Ting-a-ling was standing close to the fringe on his scarf, which lay over one end of the table.

"How I should like to go with him," said the little

fairy, and he took hold of the fringe. "But he doesn't want me, or he would take me along. I would ask him, if he would only be quiet a minute—"

Just then up jumped the Giant; and as Ting-a-ling had not let go of the fringe, he was jerked up too. He held on bravely; and as he did not wish to swing about on the scarf, he climbed up to the Giant's shoulder, and took tight hold of his long hair. With the man and his slaves in a large round basket in one hand, and his great club in the other, away went Tur-il-i-ra, with strides longer than across the street, and he walked so fast, that Ting-a-ling had to hold on tight, to keep from being blown away.

About noon they came to a large palace, surrounded by smaller dwellings; and on the porch of the palace there stood a King and a Queen and three princesses, and they were all crying. On the steps, in the grounds and gardens, and everywhere, were the lords and ladies, and common people, and they were all crying too. When these disconsolate people saw the Giant approaching, they set up a great shout of joy, and rushed to meet him, calling out, "O, the Kyrofatalapynx has broken loose!"

Tur-il-i-ra went up to the palace, and sat down on the great portico, with his feet on the ground, and the people told him (all speaking at once, and not having even manners enough to let the King have the first say) that the Kyrofatalapynx had grown awfully strong and savage since the Giant had tied him up, and that he had at last broken loose, and was now ravaging the country. He had carried off ever so many camels, and horses, and sheep, and oxen, and had threatened to eat up every person in those parts, who was under age. But since he had found out that they had sent for Tur-il-i-ra, he had gone into the forest, and they knew not when he would come forth. Then up spoke a woodman above all the clamor, and he said he knew when he would come out, for he had been in the forest that morning, and had stumbled on the Kyrofatalapynx, which was so busy making something that he did not see him; and he heard him mutter to himself, over and over again, "When he comes, I'll rush out and finish him, and then I'll be head of them all."

"All right," cried Tur-il-i-ra. "I'll wait down there by the edge of the forest; and when he sees me, he can rush out, and then you will all soon know who will be finished."

So the Giant went over to the wood, and sat down and waited. After a while, he got very sleepy, and he thought he would take a little nap until the Kyrofatalapynx should come. In order that the people might wake him up in time, he tied a long rope to one of his ear rings (his eyes had been a little weak in his youth), and everybody took hold of the end of the rope, and they promised to pull good and hard when they heard the trees crushing in the forest. So the Giant went to sleep, and the people all listened for the Kyrofatalapynx,—holding their breaths, and standing ready to jerk the rope when he should come.

Poor little Ting-a-ling was nearly consumed with curiosity. What *was* the Kyrofatalapynx? He slipped down to the ground without being noticed by anybody; and, as they all seemed so intent listening and watching, he felt afraid to speak to any of them. Directly a happy thought struck him.

"I will go into the wood myself. Whatever the Kyfymytaly-gyby is, he won't be likely to see me, and I can run and tell Tur-il-i-ra where he is, before he comes out of the wood."

So away he went, and soon was deep in the darkness of the forest. But he could hear no noise, and saw nothing that appeared to have life. Even the very birds and insects seemed to have flown away. After wandering some distance, he suddenly met a fairy, a little bit of a fellow, but somewhat larger than himself, and entirely green. Ting-a-ling spoke to him, and told him what he was after.

"That isn't exactly his name," said the green fairy, politely, "but I know what you mean. If you come this way, I can show him to you."

So Ting-a-ling followed him, and presently they came to the edge of an opening in the middle of the forest; and there, sure enough, was the Kyrofatala-pynx. With one of his great red tails coiled around an immense oak-tree, and the other around a huge rock, he sat with his elephantine legs gathered up under him, as if he were about to spring over the tree-tops. But he had no such idea. In his great hands, as big as travelling-trunks, he held a long iron bar, one end of which he was sharpening against a stone. By his side lay an immense bow, made of a tall young yew-tree, and the cord was a long and tough grape-vine. As he sat sharpening this great arrow, he grinned until his horrid teeth looked like a pale-fence around a little garden, and he muttered to himself as he worked away,—"Four hundred and nine more rubs, and I can send it twang through him; twang, twang, twang!"

"Isn't he horrid?" whispered Ting-a-ling.

"Yes, indeed," said the green fairy. "When he was young, he came out of the mouth of a volcano; and the King here, who is very fond of wonderful things, got Tur-il-i-ra to catch him, and chain him up for him in a great yard he had made for him. But now that he is grown up, no chains can hold him, and I expect he will kill the Giant with that great iron arrow, before he can come near him."

"O!" cried Ting-a-ling, "he mustn't do that. We must never let him do that!"

"We!" said the fairy, in a voice of astonishment.

"Yes, yes, I mean us. O, what shall we do? Let's cut his bowstring," said Ting-a-ling, in great excitement, and drawing his little sword. The green fairy, although polite, could not help laughing at this idea; but Ting-a-ling slipped softly to where the bow was lying, a little behind the Kyrofatalapynx, and commenced to cut away at it; but although the green fairy took the sword when he was tired, they could make but little impression on the stout grape-vine, nearly as thick as they were high.

"Let's nick the sword," said Ting-a-ling, "and then it will be a saw." And so, with a sharp little flint, they nicked the edge of it, and the edge of the green fairy's knife (for he had no sword), and as they commenced to saw away as hard as they could at the grape-vine, they heard the Kyrofatalapynx muttering, "Only three hundred and seven more rubs, and then—twang, twang, twang!"

They worked like little heroes now; and as the fairy's sword was of the sharpest steel, they cut a good way into the vine; but just when they were nearly tired out, they heard the words,—"Ninety-three more rubs, and—twang, twang, twang!"

"O, let's saw, let's saw," cried Ting-a-ling (and it's a wonder the Kyrofatalapynx did not hear him), and they worked as hard as they did at first.

"Six more rubs, and—twang, twang, twang!" cried the Kyrofatalapynx, and the two little fairies fell down exhausted and disheartened. The vine was cut but little more than half through.

Up rose the mighty creature; and with his bow and

arrow in his hands, he pushed quietly through the wood. The two fairies jumped up in a few minutes, and hurried after him; and as he went very slowly, so as not to be perceived, they reached the edge of the wood just as he crashed out into the open field.

"O!!!" shouted all the people, and they pulled the rope with a terrible jerk. Up sprang the Giant, but there stood the Kyrofatalapynx, with his long iron arrow already fitted into his bow. "Ha, ha!" he cried, "I shall put it through you—twang!" And he drew his arrow to its very head, and all the people fell down on their faces, and even Tur-il-i-ra turned a little pale. But snap! went the bowstring, and down fell the arrow! Then up rushed the Giant, and with one crushing blow of his rock-knobbed club, he laid the Kyrofatalapynx stone-dead!

The King, and the Queen, and the princesses, and all the people jumped up, and in their wild joy they would have kissed the clothes off the good Giant, had he been willing to wait.

"All right!" he cried; "I must be off. I've a friend at home waiting for me. No thanks. You can stuff him now. Good-by!"

And away he went, and poor little Ting-a-ling was left behind!

When he saw the Giant walking away like a steam-engine on stilts, Ting-a-ling began to cry.

"Did you come with him?" said the green fairy. "Well, he's gone, and you can live with me now."

But Ting-a-ling was so overcome with sorrow, and begged so hard that his new friend should tell him of some way to follow the Giant, that the latter, after thinking a while, took him up into the King's pigeon-house. Warning him to be careful not to let any of the birds pick him up, the green fairy pointed out a gray pigeon to Ting-a-ling.

"Now," said he, "if we can get a string around the middle feather of his tail, we are all right."

"How so?" asked Ting-a-ling.

"Why, then you get on, and start him off, and by pulling the string you can make him go any way you wish; for you know he steers himself with his tail."

"Good!" cried Ting-a-ling, and they both looked for a string. When they had found one, they stole up to the pigeon, who was eating corn, and tied it fast to the middle feather of his tail, without his knowing anything about it.

"Now jump on and I'll start him off," said the green fairy; and Ting-a-ling ran up the pigeon's tail (which almost touched the floor), and took his seat on its back, holding tight on to its feathers. Then the green fairy ran around the pigeon's head, and shouted in its ear, as it was pecking corn—"Hawk!"

The bird just lifted up its head, and gave one shoot right out of the window of the pigeon-house. It went high up into the air; and Ting-a-ling, when he looked around and saw which way he ought to go, pulled his string this way and that way, and he found that he could steer the pigeon very well, and even make him keep up in the air, by pulling his tail-feather straight up. So on they went, and they got to the Giant's castle before the Giant himself. The pigeon flew over the castle, but Ting-a-ling steered him back again, and backward and forward, two or three times, until the bird thought he might as well stop there; and so he alighted on the roof, and off jumped Ting-a-ling. The first thing he saw there, after the pigeon had flown away again, was the green fairy!

"Why, where did you come from?" cried Ting-a-ling.

"O," said the other, laughing, and jumping up and

down, "I thought I'd come too, and I hung on to his leg. It was nice, sitting up among his warm feathers, when his legs were curled up under him; a great deal better than being on top."

Ting-a-ling was very glad to have his friend with him, and he took him down-stairs. When the Giant got home, there they were, both in the middle of the table in the great hall, ready to welcome him. Tur-il-i-ra did not ask where the green fairy came from; but he was glad to see him, and he ordered supper to be laid on a table out on the lawn; for he was warm with his long walk. After supper, the two fairies came down to the Giant's end of the table, and he told them all that had happened, and how fortunate it was that the bowstring of the Kyrofa-talapynx had broken.

"He did it!" cried the green fairy, pointing to Ting-a-ling; and then he told the whole story of their doings, and Ting-a-ling had to explain how he had gone with the Giant. Tur-il-i-ra listened until they had quite finished, and then exclaimed, "Well! I never saw such a little thing as you are, Ting-a-ling, for being in the right place at the right time. Never, never!" And he brought his hand down on the table with such an emphatic bang, that Ting-a-ling and the green fairy shot into the air like rifle-balls. Ting-a-ling went up, up, and up, until a high wind took him, and it blew him over a river, and a wood, and a high hill, and a wide plain; and then he fell down, down, down,—right into the middle of a soft powder puff-ball, with which a lady was powdering her neck.

"Mercy on us!" cried the lady, when she saw a little fairy in the puff-ball that she was just going to put up to her throat.

"It's only I, Nerralina," cried Ting-a-ling, who immediately recognized her; "wait a minute, until I get my breath."

Sure enough, it was Nerralina, the Princess's lady, who had been on a visit to her mother, in a distant country, and returning, had ordered her slaves to pitch her tent where she now was, about half a day's journey from the palace. Ting-a-ling told his story, and they had a nice time, talking of their past adventures; and in the morning Nerralina took Ting-a-ling with her to his home in the palace gardens.

As to the green fairy, he came down in a spider web. When he got out and stood on the grass, he said, "I shall not go back to that Giant. He is good, but he is too violent."

So he went to the river and got a nice chip, and he loaded it with honeysuckles and clover blossoms, and pushed it off into the stream; he then lay down on his back in the middle of his clover, and, sucking a honeysuckle, floated away in the moonlight, down to his home, where he arrived in two or three days, just as his honeysuckles were all gone.

When Tur-il-i-ra saw what he had done, he was in great trouble indeed. He ordered all his slaves to bring their little children, and he gathered up great handfuls of them, and spread them out all over the grass, so that they might look for the two lost fairies. But of course they could not find them; and just as the sun was setting, and the Giant was going to bed in despair, there came a horseman from Nerralina, telling him that Ting-a-ling was safe, and was going home with her. Early in the morning Tur-il-i-ra went to the palace gardens, and Ting-a-ling seeing him, they went down to the wood where they were when this story opened. Tur-il-i-ra wanted Ting-a-ling to go back and finish his visit.

"No," said the fairy. "I like you very much indeed, but I'm afraid I'm most too little for your house."

"Perhaps that's true," said the Giant; "and when you want to see them, there are so many good people here in the palace. I am sure I like common human beings very much, and I would wish to be with them always, if they were not so little."

"I like them too," said Ting-a-ling, "and would live with them all the time, if they were not so big."

Afterword

Frank Stockton wrote many stories—both fairy tales and realistic fictions—but while a few remain popular to this day despite their elevated language and florid Victorian phrases—none have the impact still of "The Lady, or the Tiger?"

Originally entitled "The King's Arena," the story was written as a performance piece to be read at the dinner meeting of a literary society. The reading was more than a success. The members debated it for hours after.

The enthusiasm of his fellow club members made Stockton send the story out for publication. It was accepted by *The Century Magazine*. But while Stockton was away in Europe on a trip, the editor decided to rename the piece, cabling his decision to Stockton and publishing it in November 1882.

By the time Stockton returned to America he was a famous man. The story had engendered so much discussion and mail that he was deluged. Everyone wanted to know the same thing: did the daughter of the semi-barbaric king choose the lady or the tiger for her lover?

Debating societies spent many evenings discussing the matter. Preachers preached on it from their pulpits. It was even—so an English friend living in India reported to Stockton—mulled over by Hindu sages. An operetta based on it was produced in New

York City in 1888. And the phrase "the lady or the tiger?" entered the language as a phrase meaning an unsolvable problem.

Other writers—amateur and professional—flooded the *Century* office with sequels to the story.

At a party, Stockton was served ice cream carved in the shapes of a lady and a tiger. People jostled around waiting to see which one he would dig his spoon into first.

Stockton despaired of ever writing anything that popular again. Editors began turning down his stories, proclaiming they wanted only "another *Lady, or the Tiger.*" He finally wrote a story called "His Wife's Deceased Sister" as a kind of protest against—as he said—"the assumption that when a man does his very best he places himself under the obligation to do as well on every succeeding occasion or starve to death for lack of the ability to do so."

It took him nearly three years after the publication of "The Lady, or the Tiger?" to reestablish himself in the marketplace. But when he started getting published again, he was writing some of his very best work though, unlike "The Lady, or the Tiger?" these stories did not rely on a gimmick ending for their power. Stories like "The Bee-Man of Orn" and "The Griffin and the Minor Canon" came tumbling from him.

Yet even today the story with which he is most closely associated is the one that begins: "In the very olden time there lived a semi-barbaric king. . . ." and ends with the unsolvable question of the lady or the tiger.

—Jane Yolen